molly o'malley
rise of the changeling

molly o'malley
rise of the changeling

by
Duane Porter

cover art by
Karen Porter

Buried Treasure Publishing — Blue Springs

Molly O'Malley: Rise of the Changeling

Library of Congress Control Number 2008906638

Publisher's Cataloging-In-Publication Data
(Prepared by The Donohue Group, Inc.)

Porter, Duane.
   Molly O'Malley : rise of the changeling / by Duane Porter ; cover art by Karen Porter. -- 1st ed.

   p. : ill. ; cm. -- (Molly O'Malley ; 2)

   Summary: Molly, an eleven-year-old girl from Chicago, returns to Ireland to rescue her leprechaun friend Paddy from a prison cell. This leads them both to a mystery involving a changeling, and they uncover a threat to the entire fairy kingdom.
   ISBN-13: 978-0-9800993-1-7
   ISBN-10: 0-9800993-1-5

1. Leprechauns--Juvenile fiction. 2. Changelings--Juvenile fiction. 3. Ireland--Juvenile fiction. 4. Leprechauns--Fiction. 5. Changelings--Fiction. 6. Ireland--Fiction. I. Porter, Karen. II. Title. III. Title: Rise of the changeling

PZ7.P67 Mom 2009
[Fic]   2008906638

Published by Buried Treasure Publishing
Blue Springs MO 64015
BuriedTreasurePublishing.com

To Joannah, Caraleena, and Isabella,
the three most dedicated
Paddy Finegan fans
in the world.

Acknowledgements

When a fairy tale drifts into the realm of history, where things really happen, and then drifts back into the realm of fantasy, a writer truly prizes the work of those who have gone before. This book would not be possible without the exhaustive research of those who record both history and the classic Irish fairy tales.

A special thanks to my editors; Anita Mosley, Beth King, Linda Carrell, the Parkside Writers group, the JWKC (Juvenile Writers of Kansas City) writer's group and Cathy Porter for their editing and general comments on the story.

A tip of the tweed cap to Noel Walsh in Ireland for his help with Gaelic pronunciation.

Once again I am indebted to my daughter Karen for creating a wonderful cover and many of the interior illustrations.

contents

how to say it
in irish

Name	Pronunciation
Alvaro Giovanni	All-VAR-oh zhee-oh-VANN-ee*
Anamith	AH-nah-mih
Cathair	KAH-heer
Cillian	KILL-ee-yan
Daghda	DA-da
Dúr	DOOER
Fannléas	fon-LAY-us
Fionn	fee-YON
Fionnbharr	fee-YON-var
Gleoiteog	GLOW-teog
Lia Fáil	LEE-yah FAYL
Lioc	LEE-ock
Lugh	LOO
O'Doherty	oh DAW-har-tee
Sidhe	SHEE
Tagnus	TAHG-nuss
Tiarnach	TEER-nauk
Tuatha dé Danaan	TOO-ah dey DON-on
Vroknar	VROK-nar

Yes, you're right — this is actually an Italian name!

prologue

The Changeling

the dark figure paused at the closed door. *"Oscail,"* the raspy voice intoned, and the wooden door drifted open. With some difficulty the figure struggled in under the weight of a traveling cloak while carrying a heavy bundle wrapped in a stained blanket. Crossing the room to the fireplace, the stranger looked down into the cradle that stood by the hearth.

The baby boy within the cradle slept peacefully, warmed by the fire that was now burnt down into steady embers. His perfect features glowed with health and great possibility. He moved slightly in his sleep, too young to roll over yet, and his tiny thumb found its way to his mouth.

A grin spread across the stranger's face. She pushed her hood back revealing distinctly pointed ears. Deep wrinkles etched her face, along with a couple of warts, one sprouting some unsightly hairs. Her once-brown tresses were now faded into an ugly grey mass of fiber. A couple of teeth had gone missing, making her smile all the more hideous.

She pinched her great crooked nose with delight, then set her bundle on the hearth and peeled back the filthy blanket. A second baby cried softly as she uncovered him.

Quickly she removed the baby boy from the cradle and set him on the hearth beside the second child. She murmured some mysterious words and sprinkled a golden powder over the second baby, whose appearance changed like melting wax to nearly match that of the boy from the cradle. "Close enough," the hag muttered with satisfaction, and she laid the changed baby into the empty cradle.

Wrapping the beautiful baby boy she had stolen from the cradle in the stained blanket, she lifted him with a slight grunt and walked out the door. Tugging her hood over her head again, she whispered *"Druid."* Behind her the door closed with only a subdued click.

As she made her way into the surrounding forest, she pulled back the blanket to see the baby once again. He slept fitfully now, the rags no equal to the warm fire. "Shush," said the old fairy-woman. "It's a fine new home you'll be in soon enough." She allowed herself a low cackle that grew into a victory howl.

At the edge of a clearing a wolf heard the sound and stopped, wondering what it was. Sniffing the breeze that wafted from the direction of the disturbance, he bared his fangs and growled, his lips curled back in a snarl of disgust. Then he turned and melted into the forest shadows.

chapter one

Winter Picnic

Molly was as nervous as she was the day she had the wishes granted to her.

Her parents were getting ready for her father's Christmas party in downtown Chicago. "Molly, are you *sure* you'll be all right until we get back? It may be late." Molly's mother checked her makeup one last time in the mirror and tucked her purse under her arm.

The red-haired girl sighed loudly and rolled her eyes. "Mom, I *told* you I'll be fine. Geez, I'm going to be twelve in March."

Sean O'Malley began tugging on his leather gloves. "Kate, she'll be fine. She'll be staying inside, the doors are locked, the alarm will be on, and we *both* know she knows how to use the phone." He winked at his daughter, who screwed her face into a pout before breaking into a sly grin.

"I don't talk on the phone *that* much. But thanks for the vote of support!"

Kate O'Malley kissed her daughter lightly on the forehead and checked for lipstick marks. "We love you, dear, that's all. Is my hair okay?"

"You're gorgeous like always, Mom. Now you two get out of here and have a great time. I have a movie marathon date with the DVD player!"

The O'Malley parents stepped out into the garage. As the kitchen door closed Molly punched the security code to set the alarm. "Armed! Stay! Exit now!" a mechanical voice screeched from the security pad speaker. Molly listened for the garage door to come down and ran to the window to watch the BMW drive to the corner and turn out of the subdivision.

"At last! I thought they'd never leave!" Molly flew to the kitchen and slapped together a lunch with a ham and cheese sandwich, chips, and a couple of rosy apples. Grabbing her light jacket from the closet and a flashlight from the kitchen she raced up the steps to her room. She tossed her jacket on the bed and gathered up an unusual collection of items.

Her silver bracelet shone brightly, patterns of ivy and crescent moons lightly tracing its surface. "Paddy, I hope the enchantment you put on this lasts forever. I probably won't need it to find you this time, but I'm not going to leave it here."

Molly paused for a moment, remembering how she first met Paddy in Ireland last summer. She had gone into the Burren, a rocky wilderness of hills and ancient ruins, only to become lost in the fog. "He was so cute, sleeping there with his hammer and shoe. All two feet of him. And I didn't even know he was a leprechaun. Lucky for me! If we hadn't become friends, I might not have made it back to Aunt Shannon's!"

Molly's aunt lived on the west coastline of Ireland between the Burren and Galway Bay. The Bay stretched out to the Atlantic Ocean past the Aran Islands that lay just off the coast. Molly had become very close to her aunt in the months she spent with her.

"Ooh, I can't waste time remembering now. I only have about six hours until they get back!" She pulled her boots out of the closet. "I'll need these tonight if I do any walking in the

Burren. I sure am glad Paddy made these boots for me. Leprechauns make the best shoes in the world!" Lacing them up on her feet, she stood and felt the weight of her necklaces on her chest.

Molly pulled the silver heart-shaped locket out first. She opened it to reveal her parent's pictures framed inside, her father on the left and her mother on the right. Lying across her mother's picture was a shamrock, which surprisingly looked as fresh as the day it was picked in midsummer.

Closing her eyes, Molly allowed herself to remember that night, that wonderful, frightening night, when the fairies danced in a circle like huge glowing fireflies around Paddy and her, dancing under the full moon until they vanished in a blaze of blue light. Then Paddy had cast the spell that granted Molly three wishes that were stored in this very shamrock. Those wishes had real power and carried a heavy responsibility.

She remembered her first wish, to find the unknown thief who had stolen the leprechauns' gold. The glowing green light from the shamrock had led them to an underground cave where it revealed a black fire-breathing dragon lying on the golden treasure.

When no other solution seemed possible, she made her second wish to solve the problem of the black dragon. And a *white* dragon appeared out of nowhere! "Stanley," Molly whispered. "I summoned you from your wonderful world of Ellesyndria to help us. And you did!" Molly felt her eyes well up as she recalled the wonderful white dragon who breathed ice instead of fire. It was Stanley who helped them understand …

Nefra. Molly closed the heart locket and pulled out the second necklace she wore. A heavier necklace, with a medallion carved from stone suspended on a golden chain. The medallion was a parting gift from Nefra, the black dragon. Nefra and Stanley had fallen in love. The gold had been returned to the leprechauns, and all was well. Except …

The reason Molly was in Ireland in the first place was because her father was paying more attention to his work than he was to his family. Her mother had gone into the hospital suffering from exhaustion, and her father, unable — or unwilling — to juggle everything at once, decided to send Molly to Ireland for the summer to stay with his sister, Shannon. Molly was desperate to see her family solidly back together again, and she had one last wish ...

In the end, Molly chose to use her final wish to send the dragons back to safety in Ellesyndria. It was a brave choice, a noble choice. Molly's father decided to choose his family over his work in the end, too. Molly had hope once again that everything would be fine.

Molly slid her top dresser drawer open. A folded piece of worn, blackened cloth lay on the shelf bottom. It was the band that held the medallion in place around Nefra's large neck for hundreds of years until Molly untied it. "I don't think I'll need this," Molly decided. She pushed the cloth to one side, revealing a weathered leather pouch.

Setting the pouch carefully on the dresser top, Molly loaded her lunch into a backpack, pulled on her jacket, and looked into the mirror. A pretty girl with deep green eyes, slightly bushy shoulder-length red hair and a splash of freckles stared back at her. She smiled at the image. "Are you ready for an adventure, Molly O'Malley?" she asked her reflection.

The last time she had used the pouch was right after she had returned from Ireland. It was yet another gift from Paddy — "That leprechaun spoils me!" — given with strict instructions not to open it until she was back home. The pouch contained a single gold coin that showed a woodland scene on one side, and mountains on the other. When she pulled it out of the pouch, instead of the gold disappearing as she expected leprechaun gold to do after being given away, she found herself magically transported to Ireland, right to where

Paddy Finegan, the mischievous leprechaun sat admiring the Burren sunset over the Bay of Galway.

Paddy explained that when she pulled the coin out of the pouch and thought of Paddy and old Eire — the Irish name for Ireland — she would be pulled to wherever he was. When she wanted to go back, she needed only to put the coin back into the pouch and she would return.

Molly could not stay that time, as no one knew she had gone — not that anyone would believe her, anyway — and she needed to spend time with her parents. She wanted to make sure that her father had truly mended his ways.

She had hugged the leprechaun goodbye, and returned to her room as rapidly as she had come to Eire. She kept the pouch safe, hidden deep in her drawer, until the time was right to use it again.

That time was now.

Her father had been positively doting on his wife and Molly, taking a regional job that allowed him to spend more time with his family and less time traveling. Molly's mom let him take over more of the work around the house. Kate O'Malley was much more relaxed now, and smiled a great deal more.

It was winter in Ireland too, but it would not be as cold as Chicago. Ireland was warmed by the Gulf Stream that sent ocean currents heated in the Gulf of Mexico to bathe the little island. Her jacket should be enough to handle the mild Irish winter, though Ireland could get downright blustery, even in the summer.

Her father's office Christmas party turned out to be an early present for Molly, a perfect opportunity to get both parents out of the house. No one would be checking on Molly for a whole six hours. Molly checked her clock — okay, five hours and forty minutes. Just enough time to pop over to Eire and chat with her dearest friend, Paddy Finegan the leprechaun.

She took a deep breath, held the pouch close, and drew out the golden coin. It glittered under her room's overhead light, and then went dark as she felt the sensation of floating. "It *is* the middle of the night over in Ireland, after all. I would expect it to be dark," Molly whispered to herself. The ground beneath her became solid again, and she blinked to adjust to the dim light.

The ground was stone, but it was not the Burren. She found herself in a room, built of stones mortared together. It smelled dank and musty. A dim light reflected on a wall, the source blocked by a corner. As she made her way carefully toward the light, she brushed something with her shoulder that clinked, the sound of metal against metal. Startled, she jumped back. "Silly. You have a flashlight." She pulled out the plastic tube, clicked the switch on and surveyed the wall. Swaying gently from their sockets, iron manacles hung on chains, their shadows distorted and spooky in the light.

Molly clapped her hand over her mouth to keep from crying out. These manacles were empty. But there might be others. Where was she? And more importantly, where was …

"Paddy?" she whispered. "Paddy, are … are you here?"

She listened, almost hoping there would be no answer. It would be better not to find her friend here. Not here …

Clink.

Trembling, she stepped around the corner and pointed her flashlight at the sound. A rat, surprised at the intrusion, jumped off the ledge and ran across the floor to disappear into a pile of something. Molly didn't want to know *what.*

"A rat." Molly closed her eyes and exhaled. "At least it wasn't Paddy."

"Molly?"

She froze at the voice behind her. Saying a silent prayer, she turned her flashlight in the direction of the voice.

A small man, no more than two feet tall, sat on a bench across the room. His red workman's shirt was stained and dirty, and his black hair looked unkempt and matted from neglect. His buckled shoes reflected the light like two small beacons against the bare walls. And most appallingly, miniature shackles bound his wrists and ankles.

He raised his head and looked at the girl with blood-shot eyes. "Molly O'Malley? Oh, Molly, me dear, put the coin back into the pouch and go back home as quick as ye can. Save yourself, and don't think o' your wretched Paddy ever again. Save yourself, dear child!"

chapter two

Hard Time

O f course Molly did nothing of the sort. She flew across the room and hugged the little man as if she would never let him go. "Paddy! Oh, Paddy, what have they done to you? Are you all right?"

"I'm fine at the moment, Molly dear, but ye need to get back home right now! There's nuttin' can be done for me now. Do as I say, leave me and —" his voice broke slightly — "and don't look for me again. I'll not see ye harmed by any o' my doin'."

Molly sat down on the narrow bench, wiping her tears. "I'm not leaving until you tell me exactly what is going on! What have you gotten yourself into now, Paddy Finegan?"

Paddy sighed. "If I tell ye, will ye promise to leave?"

Molly smiled. "No. But I promise that I won't leave until you tell me!"

"Stubborn girl," the leprechaun grunted. "But then, ye always did stand by your friends. Even when it wasn't the easiest thing to do."

"You're wasting time, Paddy." Molly leaned back against the stone wall and crossed her arms. "Now what is this place, and why are you here?"

The leprechaun closed his eyes in resignation. "This is the fairy prison in Donegal. I'm scheduled to be transferred to the palace dungeon any day now. I'll likely not be seein' the fair hills of Eire for two hundred years."

"Paddy! What could you have done to be punished like that? Did you kill someone?"

"Worse." He opened his eyes to look at the girl. "I — borrowed somethin'."

"You mean you stole something. Still, it couldn't be *that* bad."

Paddy winced. "I stole somethin' from the Fairy Queen herself."

"What? What could be so important that they would lock you up for two hundred years?"

A tear trickled down the elf's face. "A wee golden coin."

Molly stared at the leprechaun, then at the golden coin she still clutched in her hand. "This — this coin belongs to the Fairy Queen?"

"Aye."

"And you stole it?"

"Aye."

"Why did you do such a stupid thing?"

Paddy stretched out his arms as far as the chains would allow. "Because I had to be able to see ye, Molly. You're the best true friend this poor leprechaun ever had."

Molly looked at the coin again and placed it carefully in her pocket. She stood up and walked toward the light peeking through the cell door.

"Molly, what isit you're doin'?"

"I'm looking for a way to get you out of here." She stood on tiptoe, peering through the barred window set high on the heavy wooden door. "Oh, there they are."

"Molly, I've told ye the truth! Ye need to be puttin' that coin back into the pouch and go back home!" The leprechaun strained against his chains.

"Stop moving around, you're making too much noise. There *are* guards in this place, aren't there?" Molly pointed the flashlight into her backpack and began rummaging through its contents.

"O' course there're guards! They're goblins, and mean ones, too! What are ye doin'?"

"Hmmm … I know I packed it in here somewhere. Oh, *here* it is!" Triumphantly she emerged holding a small plastic disk.

Paddy looked at her in amazement. "Are ye crazy, girl? What is that?"

"It's my hairbrush. I try to carry one with me all the time now. You know how my hair gets if I don't keep it brushed out." She flipped the brush open. A quick push in the center, and dozens of soft rubber spikes popped out.

Paddy shook his head. "Now I *know* you're crazy. You're brushing your hair at a time like this?"

"Well, I have to look presentable if the guards show up." She reached through the bars, holding out the hairbrush. "Nope, I was afraid that wasn't going to be long enough."

"Molly, what in thunder are ye doin'? I've been in here for a couple o' months, but you've lost it in five minutes!"

Molly looked back toward Paddy, shining her flashlight in his direction. "I'm trying not to ignore you, Paddy, but I'm rather busy right now. There it is; they had to have *something* for you to use."

Paddy looked wide-eyed as the girl approached him. "Molly, are you all right?"

She stopped and shone her light into the bucket sitting next to the elf. "Well, at least it's been emptied in the last day or so. This stuff really stinks!"

"Molly, that's —"

"I know what it is, Paddy. Even leprechauns have to go to the bathroom sometime." She carefully carried the bucket to the far corner of the cell.

"Molly — what are ye — ye wouldn't — oooh!"

Molly dumped the contents of the bucket onto the floor, being careful not to splash any of the waste onto her clothes or boots. A smell stronger than a Johnny-On-The-Spot with the lid up floated across the cell. "Too bad they can't afford indoor plumbing for the prisoners," she said, coughing. As Molly walked back toward the cell door she gave Paddy a wink, shining the flashlight under her chin so he'd be sure to see it.

"It's stark raving mad she's gone, there's no doubt of it," Paddy whispered.

With a clunk, she turned the bucket upside down on the floor just under the barred window. Carefully she stepped up on top of the bucket and stretched her arm through the bars, holding her hairbrush. "That's better," she murmured, and a small clinking sound could be heard out in the corridor. "Just a little further — got it!"

She pulled her arm slowly back through the bars. Hanging on the rubber spikes of her hairbrush was a ring of metal keys.

Paddy stared at her in disbelief as she came near.

"I guess they thought no one inside could reach these, because the prisoners were chained to the walls. But they didn't count on someone else getting in. Of course, not everyone has —" she pulled the gold coin from her pocket and waved it under his nose — "a coin from the Fairy Queen."

He gulped. "M-Molly … are ye mad at me, darlin'?"

Molly calmly put the coin back in her pocket and began looking through the keys. "Why, Paddy, why would you think that I was mad at you? All you did was steal someone else's property. The Fairy Queen's property, no less. Next I imagine you added a special enchantment, and then passed it off to a dear friend as though it were a gift from you personally. *And you didn't even warn me about the danger to either of us?!*" She raised her voice at the end and glared at the tiny leprechaun. He trembled at her rage, making his chains rattle.

"What were you thinking, Paddy? Oh, I remember, you weren't thinking! The only reason you could come up with is that you wanted a friend to visit! Well, here I am! Are you happy now?" Her green eyes filled with tears.

"Molly, dear, don't be cryin' now, it's all me own fault, I know! Oh, Molly, what has Paddy done to ye?"

She blinked back her tears. "Just shut up for a minute, will you? I'm trying to find the key. Here, this one looks like it might work." She inserted a small key into the lock on Paddy's wrist manacle and twisted it. With a rusty squeak of protest, it fell open.

"Molly, you're a genius, ye are!" Paddy rubbed his wrist gratefully.

"Give the genius your other wrist, will you? We need to get you out of these things."

Soon Paddy was free and they sat side-by-side on the little bench. "Now what?" Paddy asked.

"Now we see if we can use one of these keys to unlock the front door. We'll just take you out the same way you came in." Molly stood up and walked toward the cell door, looking through the keys again.

A door creaked somewhere down the corridor. Molly stopped, holding her breath. Voices echoed through the halls, and they sounded like they were getting closer.

"The guards!" Paddy hissed. "If they come here, it's the end for both of us! Get away from the door, Molly, and see if they pass by!"

Molly stepped back into the shadows with the leprechaun and waited. Soon new shadows came through the bars, created by a moving torch.

"Hey, wasn't the keys hanging right here?" a rough voice asked.

"That's where I left 'em, I did!"

"Well, they ain't here now. You must o' left 'em somewhere else."

"No, I left 'em hangin' right here, I tell ye!"

"Let's go get the master keys and check the cells. Something fishy's goin' on here, and I'm not goin' to take the fall for it!"

The footsteps and torchlight faded into the distance. "Molly," Paddy whispered, "they'll be back in a few minutes. You've got to put the coin back into the pouch and go home! Bless ye for your kindness, but it's only you I'm thinkin' of! Please, Molly!"

Molly looked at Paddy for a moment in the semi-darkness. "Okay," she finally said, "I'll do it. I don't have a choice, do I? Those guards are coming back." Already they could hear the voices approaching again. "Paddy, I'm really sorry."

Paddy was crying now, more emotional than Molly had ever seen him. "No, Molly, I'm the one who's sorry. I've made a bloody mess of everything. Save yourself, and just try to remember the good times we had!"

He was interrupted by a face at the door, looking through the bars. "Hey, who are ye talkin' to in there? Cripes! There's somebody else in there with 'im! Get this door open, now!"

Molly turned to Paddy one last time. "I guess it's time to go," she whispered. She drew the golden coin from her pocket, holding the old leather pouch in her other hand. "I really am sorry, too, Paddy!" She knelt down and hugged the leprechaun, looked Paddy straight in the eyes, and grinned.

He knew at once what she planned. "No, Molly, don't —"

Molly dropped the coin into the pouch.

Seconds later the door burst open and three huge goblins wearing chain mail armor charged in, waving their torches and clubs. All they saw was a golden haze that lingered for only a moment.

chapter three

The White City

The wooden floor became solid under Molly and Paddy, who were still locked in their embrace. "We did it, Paddy!" Molly exclaimed. "You're free!"

Paddy pushed himself out of her arms and sat back. "What have ye done, Molly?"

Molly smiled. "I rescued you, that's what I've done!" Her smile faded as she looked around her. "Uh-oh. Paddy — this isn't exactly my bedroom."

The floor beneath them rolled slightly from side to side as Paddy shakily climbed to his feet. Vibrations rumbled through the wood boards. " 'This isn't exactly me bedroom.' Sure and you're right this isn't your bedroom! Where have ye taken us?"

Molly walked to the nearby rail and looked over it into the water. The surface was fairly smooth, and a wake trailed from their boat scattering frothy bubbles behind them. Machinery hummed and chugged beneath them, pushing them through the water at a leisurely pace. "We're on a *boat!* Paddy, how did we get on a boat?"

Before the leprechaun could answer, a portly man wearing a crisp white suit and a full mustache stepped around the corner of the cabin. He stopped when he saw Molly and Paddy. "Hullo, there, I didn't notice you youngsters earlier! Are you going to the Exposition?"

Molly and Paddy looked at each other for help. "I — I'm not sure, sir," Molly stammered. "We were just talking about where to go next."

"Oh, where are my manners? I haven't introduced myself! Daniel H. Burnham, at your service!" He swept off his white straw hat and bowed low. "Where might you two be from?"

"Eire," replied Paddy without thinking. Molly shot him a sharp look, but it was too late.

"Ireland? You're truly from Ireland? Oh this is wonderful! How do they put it over there — that's grand! I can't believe my good fortune!"

Molly stepped between the man and Paddy. "I won't let you hurt him, so don't even try!"

Burnham looked at her quizzically for a moment, and then burst into laughter. "Oh, no, my dear, you mistake me! I don't believe in leprechauns, not one bit! But he could certainly play the part," he winked broadly at Paddy, "and you *have* come to the Exposition — on Irish day, of all days!"

"What is this Exposition ye keep talking about?" Paddy asked.

Burnham thrust his finger to point at the front of the boat. "There! Lying just beyond the Peristyle! The World's Columbian Exposition, hosted by the grand people of Chicago!"

"Chicago?!" Molly whirled to look. The boat was approaching a pier that jutted out into the water. Behind it stood an impressive array of white columns, connected in the center by a huge arch. Beyond that she could see golden domes and curved roofs in the distance.

"This is the *Chicago* Exposition? The Chicago World's Fair?" She turned to Burnham, who was smiling back at her.

"The *Columbian* Exposition, to celebrate the four hundredth anniversary of Columbus' journey of discovery to this new world. Also known as the Chicago World's Fair of 1893!"

Molly leaned against the side rail for support. "1893?" She looked at Paddy for confirmation. "Paddy, we — we traveled back in *time?*"

"I'm just as confused as ye are, Molly," the elf admitted. "But I tried to warn ye ..."

"The Exposition is timeless! We have exhibits from all over the world! We showcase America's superiority in technology and agriculture here! And you have never seen architecture to compare to ..." Burnham paused to catch his breath. "My apologies, again. You see, I am the chief architect and planner for the Exposition. Please, let me be your host for the day. And you must call me 'Uncle Dan,' that's what young Frank calls me. It must be fate, meeting two people from Ireland on today of all days!"

Molly stared at the man in the white suit. "You designed all of this?"

"With the able help of the most talented architects, sculptors and artists ever assembled! True, we did take longer than planned to build it, but it was worth the wait!"

Molly nodded her head. "That's right; four hundred years would be 1892, not 1893. We learned the rhyme in school:

> *'Columbus sailed the ocean blue*
> *In fourteen hundred ninety-two.'*

It took you a whole extra year to build it?"

Uncle Dan grinned as he put his hat back on. "Well, from October to May! But we had the delightful summer months for the Exposition instead of winter. You *will* be my honored guests?"

Molly took Paddy aside and whispered, "What do you think? We don't even know him!"

"I say let's take a chance." Paddy whispered back. "Maybe he'll get us somethin' to eat."

Paddy shrugged and nodded to Uncle Dan. "May as well. It's the best offer we've had today."

The boat nudged the dock gently as men hurled lines to the pier. Within minutes the boat lay securely tied to the iron cleats. The boarding ramp quickly bridged the narrow gap to the pier, allowing the passengers to go ashore.

"So this is Lake Michigan?" Molly asked as Uncle Dan helped her step on to the pier.

"Yes, it is, young lady." Uncle Dan replied. "Good heavens! I've done it again! I haven't asked your names yet!"

"I'm Molly, and this is Paddy," Molly pointed.

"Very well, then! Molly and Paddy, follow me!"

Uncle Dan strode confidently down the pier to a place where people from the boat were lining up. He waved Molly and Paddy to the side, and walked up to a different gate.

"Good morning, Mr. Burnham," said a young lady sitting in a booth.

"Good morning! Would you be so kind as to give me two daily admission tickets for my friends, here?"

"Of course, sir!" She handed two slips of paper to the chief architect.

"Ah! Now you're set!" Uncle Dan handed Molly and Paddy each a ticket. It looked rather like money, Molly thought, as though it had been engraved. 'World's Columbian Exposition' curved across the top in large, old-English letters. Then the words 'Expressly For' lay below them, with 'Irish

Day' on the left side and 'September 30, 1893' on the right. A harp graced the lower middle part of the ticket.

"It's really true," Molly whispered. "This *is* 1893."

"Jack!" Uncle Dan's voice boomed. A young man looking not yet twenty hurried over. "Do me a favor, Jack, and pop over to the Irish Village right away. We need a proper suit for my friend Paddy, here." He gestured to the leprechaun standing behind him. "We'll be at the Administration Building shortly."

Paddy looked down at his stained and wrinkled clothes. "Aye," he grinned, "I do look a mess, don't I?"

Jack stared at Paddy for a moment, as if sizing him up. Then he nodded and ran off.

"Now, my friends, let's have a look at the Great Basin!" Uncle Dan led the way up the steps to the towering arch, which seemed to rise at least fifty feet over their heads. "This is the Peristyle," Uncle Dan said, "the grand entrance where visitors enter from the pier." They emerged on the other side and stopped to take in the view.

A huge reflecting pool filled with water stretched out before them, shadowed from the early morning light at their backs. A golden statue of a woman towered a hundred feet from the water, poised on a pedestal forty feet high. She faced away from them, but they could see that her left hand raised a staff of some sort, while her right lifted an orb with an eagle perched on top. Along the length of the basin lay mammoth buildings, built with columns and decorated with detailed carvings. Great domes rose above the rooflines. At the far end of the basin was an imposing square building capped with an awe-inspiring golden dome that sparkled in the new sun. All of the buildings were uniformly white, almost brilliantly so.

"Behold," said Uncle Dan with great pride, "the White City."

Molly could not speak as she took in the panorama. The scale and size of the buildings was breathtaking. It was evident that a great deal of planning had been done to make the different buildings seem like they all belonged here together.

They strolled together down the south side of the Great Basin. "That statue is awesome!" Molly remarked as they walked past it.

"The Statue of the Republic," Uncle Dan nodded. "The symbol of our nation, captured in classic form. Impressive, isn't she?"

"That's not real gold, is it?" Paddy casually asked.

"100% pure gold leaf, thirty-five thousand dollars of it," Uncle Dan replied proudly. "Covers all of her except her head and arms, which were left white."

Paddy whistled. "Now there's somethin' to write home about."

Molly nudged the elf and whispered, "I thought that getting home is what we needed to do. Why are we taking this tour?"

Uncle Dan overheard her and exclaimed, "But you just arrived from Ireland! Why would you want to return so soon?"

"I'm actually from Chicago," Molly sighed. "I was just visiting Ireland when we had to leave." She glared at the leprechaun, who shrugged his shoulders sheepishly.

"Then you *are* home!" boomed Uncle Dan. "You're here at the greatest moment in Chicago's proud history! Where else could you possibly think of going at a momentous time like this?"

"I'm not sure of any place else I could go right now," Molly said. She added to herself, *but I'm going to find out. I'm not giving up on going back to my real home. I just got my family back together, and I'm not going to lose them again!*

The building to their left towered above them. "This is the Agriculture Building. Its glass dome is 100 feet wide and 130 feet tall. Each building is sixty feet exactly to the cornice," Uncle Dan announced. "The architectural style is a classical form that people are calling Beaux-Arts, after the École des Beaux-Arts school in Paris that trains architects in this style. The name simply means 'School of Fine Arts'."

"What is a cornice?" Molly asked.

"A cornice is the horizontal dividing line that separates the main walls from that which lies above it. You see the columns that go up to that slab that sticks out?"

"Yes," Molly nodded, trying not to yawn.

"That slab, along with the molding and the carvings that run along with it, are what make up the cornice. It offers the eye a break so that we can do something very different above the cornice line, like place a dome or a curved roof, and it doesn't look so very much out of place."

Ahead they could see smaller canals branching off to the north and south sides of the reflecting pool. Ornate bridges allowed visitors to cross the canals. Uncle Dan continued his talk. "Everything surrounding the Grand Basin is known as the Court of Honor. Mark this, my friends; make no little plans. They have no magic to stir men's blood and probably will not themselves be realized, I always say."

"What is *in* all of these buildings?" Molly asked.

"Mostly exhibits of various sorts. There are two models of the Liberty Bell here, one made of oranges, and the other of wheat, oats and rye. The real Liberty Bell is on display in the Pennsylvania building, of course."

"Right here at the Fair?" Molly shook her head. "This is incredible."

"What's in this next building?" Paddy asked, as they crossed the canal.

"Ah, Machinery Hall. Truly a marvel that shows America's technology to the world. In here we have Eli Whitney's cotton gin, the world's largest conveyer belt, sewing machines — and of course the Fair's power plant."

"Sounds boring," Molly groaned.

Uncle Dan laughed. "We even have some of the equipment on display that was used to cast the axle for the Ferris Wheel."

"Ferris wheel? You have a Ferris wheel here?" Molly asked with some interest.

"I should say not!" Uncle Dan's eyes bulged with mild shock. "We have *the* Ferris Wheel here, the first and only one in the world! Why, Mr. Ferris came up with the idea for his wheel while dining at a chop house in Chicago after we were already building all of this!" He indicated the Court of Honor with a broad sweep of his arm. "He conceived the idea, the technical details of its support spokes, the manner of loading and even the number of revolutions it would make, all on the spot! Then he built it with no modifications, and it works splendidly! The man's a marvel!"

"Cool! Can we see the Ferris Wheel?"

"Of course you can, Molly my dear. You *must* see it. It's the most exciting thing on the Midway! It hasn't been up long, it just opened about three months ago, but it has already paid for itself. First, though, we must make a stop at the Administration Building."

They reached the far end of the Great Basin, where multiple fountains sprayed water on statues of horses rising out of the water. A central fountain surrounded a fourteen foot statue of Christopher Columbus. Uncle Dan led them to toward the large square building with the beautiful golden dome. They could see now that the dome had eight sides.

"How tall is this dome?" Paddy murmured as he strained to look up.

"Two hundred fifty feet, my small friend," Uncle Dan called back. "Let's step inside to my office for a moment."

They entered through a beautiful doorway that was fifty feet wide and fifty feet high. Uncle Dan led them up a staircase as Molly and Paddy followed close behind. At last they arrived at a door labeled 'Director of Works.'

"Let's sit here for a few minutes. Jack should be here soon, he's a good lad." Uncle Dan entered and found a seat behind a large mahogany desk, waving Molly and Paddy to two wooden chairs that stood in the office. "How long are you staying, children?" the director asked, as he set his straw hat on the corner of his desk.

"I — I really don't know yet." Molly shook her head. "We just got here, and everything is very confusing right now. Things have been happening so *fast.*"

"My life for the past year and a half," Uncle Dan grunted. "But everything is working out! We expect to top twenty-seven million visitors to the Exposition by the time it ends next month!"

A light knock sounded at the door. "Come in," called Uncle Dan.

The young man from the pier stuck his head in. "I got it, Mr. Burnham."

"Excellent!" Uncle Dan went to the door and accepted a large paper bag. "Thank you Jack, I knew I could count on you!" Jack smiled and nodded as he hurried off.

"Now, my fine leprechaun, let's see what we have for you." He reached into the bag and pulled out a green top hat with a buckle on the band.

"By the stars! Did he get the full outfit, then?" Paddy's face glowed with excitement.

Uncle Dan proceeded to pull out green trousers, a clean white shirt, a light green vest and an emerald-green waistcoat.

There was even a matching bow-tie. "Why don't you try these on for size? You can use my bathroom to clean yourself up and get dressed. You look like you've had a rough day."

"Ye don't know the half of it, sir! Bless ye!" Paddy eagerly grabbed the clothes and stepped into the bathroom, closing the door behind him.

"Thank you, Mr. Burnham — I mean, Uncle Dan, for everything you've done for us! I don't know where we would be if you hadn't helped us on the boat!" Molly smiled and allowed herself to relax for the first time in hours. "Oh, look, you can see right across the Great Basin to the Statue of the Republic from your window. Then the Peristyle is behind that, and then Lake Michigan ..." She shook her head. "It's still hard to believe we're here."

Uncle Dan grinned. "The Exposition is a magical place where anything can happen, Molly!"

Molly turned to look at him. "Excuse me, what did you say?"

"I said that the Exposition is a magical place where anything can happen. Why?"

At that moment the bathroom door opened and Paddy Finegan stepped into the room. The new clothes fit him perfectly, and his hair was clean and combed. Even the grime from his prison stay was scrubbed away. He looked as fine as he did the night he cast the wishes spell on Molly several months ago — or was it a hundred years from now? Molly shook her head again. This was way too confusing.

"Now there's a true leprechaun if ever I saw one!" Uncle Dan chortled. "Paddy, you look magnificent!"

"I do feel much better, and thank ye for the compliment!" Paddy bowed low and gave Molly a wink. "What do we do next?"

"There's only one thing to do, of course!" Uncle Dan stood up and retrieved his straw hat. "We're going to Ireland!"

chapter four

A Bit o' the Green

Ireland?" Molly wasn't sure she could handle any more surprises today. "How can we go to Ireland?"

"It's a nice day. I think we'll walk." Uncle Dan smiled at her as he donned his hat. "I'm sorry, Molly, I couldn't resist having a bit of fun with you! Nations from all over the world have exhibits at the Exposition, and the Emerald Isle is no exception. There are two remarkable Irish exhibits on the Midway Plaisance that I'm sure you will approve of. And you as well, Paddy!"

"What are they?" Paddy asked.

"Could I describe the Court of Honor to you? No, my friends, some things you have to experience to get the full effect. Trust me, the Irish have done themselves proud."

Uncle Dan led Molly and Paddy out of the Administration Building, where they turned to walk along the North Canal. Molly caught one last glimpse of the Statue of the Republic standing at the far end of the reflecting pool, flanked by the majestic Peristyle behind the golden lady. Then the scene was blocked by the stately buildings of the White City as they left the Court of Honor.

Soon they approached a natural lagoon surrounding wooded areas. Foot bridges spanned the water to reach the other side, where families ambled down shaded paths. "That is Wooded Island," Uncle Dan indicated as they passed by. "It's very popular on hot days. You can escape the heat under a big shade tree, have a picnic, or just relax after walking all day. The Exposition is a big place; you really can't see it all in one day."

"Speakin' o' picnics, can we get somethin' to eat? I haven't had a decent meal in weeks." Paddy looked hopefully at their white-suited benefactor.

"Of course, Paddy, of course! I know just the place on the Midway, which is where we're headed now. Can you hold out for another half-hour or so?"

"He's tough," Molly answered for him. "You'll be all right, won't you, Paddy?"

Paddy sighed and managed a grin. "I feel much better now than I did just a few hours ago, that's a fact. I can wait another half-hour."

Passing by Wooded Island they neared a large building to their left. This was not the same type of building that they saw in the White City. Instead, this building had all sorts of different colors: reds, oranges, and yellows. Molly thought they all combined for a very modern look.

In the center was a huge entryway, made of a series of receding arches that shone as if they were made from gold. Uncle Dan pointed it out as they walked by it. "This is the Transportation Building, with its famous Golden Door! It's not my favorite piece of architecture, but then Louis Sullivan has different ideas than I do on what great architecture should be."

A man's voice spoke from behind them. "Perhaps you should pay more attention to Louis Sullivan, Uncle Dan, instead of clinging to the outdated architecture of the past."

The group turned to see a young man in his mid twenties reclining on a park bench.

"Frank! It's good to see you, boy! My goodness, I didn't expect to see you here again, after your remarks this summer!" In an aside to Molly and Paddy he whispered, "This is young Frank I've been telling you about!" Uncle Dan walked over to the bench and grasped Frank's hand firmly, lifting him to his feet before clasping him in a great bear hug.

"Frank, you must meet some new friends of mine. This is Molly and Paddy, who have recently arrived from Ireland! Ireland, isn't that remarkable, on today of all days?" Frank smiled and nodded politely. "Molly, Paddy, may I introduce to you Frank Lloyd Wright."

Molly was just taking Frank's extended hand. She froze. "Frank Lloyd Wright? *The* Frank Lloyd Wright? The architect?!"

"Some consider me an architect, yes," Frank replied with a twinkle in his eye, giving Uncle Dan a wink.

"Frank's a fine architect, no doubt about that," Uncle Dan smiled. "He just spends too much time with Sullivan pursuing this modern nonsense."

"I sort of like the Transportation Building. It's different." Molly stared into Frank's eyes for a moment, then she turned and looked at Uncle Dan. "But I loved the White City, too! Just in a different sort of way."

"There, uncle, we have a true connoisseur of the arts among us. Someone who can appreciate both of our worlds." Frank smiled as Molly finally released his hand.

"What is a connoisseur?" Molly asked.

"A connoisseur is a discerning judge of the best in any field. Someone who plays with more than one string on their guitar." Frank smiled at Uncle Dan again. "Someone who can build something newer than what Rome offered."

Uncle Dan rested his hand on Frank's shoulder. "Frank, the Exposition has been a resounding success. Even you must admit that."

"Oh, I agree completely, Uncle. It's been *too* successful. You know that Sullivan has said that the success of the White City in capturing people's imaginations will set American architecture back fifty years?"

"Yes, I had heard that," Uncle Dan chuckled. "Sour grapes. The classic architecture and our new emphasis on city planning will dominate public and corporate building projects for decades to come."

Frank shook his head sadly. "Barren, empty, symmetrical white buildings that stamp their design on nature. This used to be a park, Uncle! Now we have rows of white stucco blotting out the horizon! Buildings should complement nature and stand in harmony with it, not overwhelm it!"

"This place was a swamp before we started. It was fit only for mosquitoes, not for children. Now we have built something beautiful here, something all the world can see." Uncle Dan spoke softly but firmly.

Frank sighed. "As always, we must agree to disagree." He turned to Molly and Paddy. "I'm pleased to have met you. I'm sorry we had to air our differences in front of you, but don't mind Uncle Dan here. He really is a loveable old cuss." Frank shook Uncle Dan's hand one last time. "Even if he doesn't like modern architecture."

"Oh, go build something memorable," Uncle Dan said fondly.

Frank walked away to the south as the trio continued north. The morning sun peeked through the occasional clouds. Paddy looked over to see Molly staring at her hand.

"Molly," he grinned, "you're going to have to wash that hand sometime."

Molly looked up in surprise, and then she smiled. "Oh — I know, Paddy. I just want to savor the moment right now. Young Frank is going to be very famous some day."

"In just a few minutes you're going to be savoring something quite different," Uncle Dan said. "We'll walk around the back of the Women's Building here to reach the Midway and Paddy's lunch."

Molly stopped without warning, staring into the distance. "Is something wrong, Molly?" Uncle Dan asked.

"That building over there, beyond these ponds ..."

"Yes?"

"I know that building."

"That is the Fine Arts Building. We have an extensive collection of artwork for the Exposition on display there."

Molly shook her head. "No, there is something else about it. Where have I ..." She snapped her fingers. "I've got it! That's the Museum of Science and Industry! I've been there with my class from school!"

Uncle Dan looked at Molly in amazement. "The Columbian Museum of Chicago plans to take over the building after the Exposition closes, but they organized only two weeks ago! They plan to preserve art, archeology, science and industry, as I recall. How the devil did you know about that?"

"Lucky guess, I suppose!" Paddy said cheerily. He tugged Molly's arm so that she bent close and whispered so only she could hear. "Molly, if we really have traveled back in time, we must be careful not to change history. Just react to everything as if it was new to ye."

Molly nodded and shrugged her shoulders. "Yeah, lucky guess," she said loudly, and smiled.

They continued past the Women's Building and crossed under the railroad tracks. A banner attached to the bridge read "Welcome to the Midway Plaisance!" Molly felt the mood change immediately as festive music played. This was more like a carnival atmosphere, very different from the pomp and grandeur of the White City.

"What is the Midway?" Molly questioned.

"The Midway is a unique part of the Exposition. There are rides here like the Ice Slide, the Ferris Wheel of course, and others. There are games of chance and skill. There are shows that reveal the strange and odd. There are even a few shows that children should not watch. That hootchie-kootchie dancer from Egypt, for example. All exhibits here seem bent on taking as much money out of visitors' pockets as quickly as possible. Even so, the people seem to enjoy it!"

Uncle Dan pointed to a small building. "Last but not least, there are many places in the Midway where a hungry or thirsty traveler can buy food or quench their thirst! Here we are, Paddy, a treat for our special visitor from Ireland!" Uncle Dan led them to a window where a sign read 'A. L. Feuchtwanger Sausages and Meats.' He stuck his head inside and called out, "Anton! It's Burnham, my dear fellow! Three of your famous sausages, please!"

A man with dark curly hair and a mustache walked over behind the counter. "Mr. Burnham!" he said cheerfully. "How nice to see you again!" He called over his shoulder, "Henry, three sausages for Mr. Burnham, pronto!"

Uncle Dan laid some coins on the counter. Molly noticed that one of them had a picture of Christopher Columbus on it. "Uncle Dan, is that real money?"

"Of course, my dear! This is a fifty-cent piece minted specially for the Exposition by the United States Government! It's the first time that has ever been done, I believe. I received a proof coin, which is of higher quality than the rest of the coins produced. I really shouldn't be carrying it around in my pocket. The rest are being sold for a dollar each as collector items."

Anton handed three pairs of white gloves to Uncle Dan, who gave one pair to Molly and a smaller pair, still much too large, to Paddy. Uncle Dan pulled his gloves on, so they did the same.

"Three sausages, here you go!" Anton used tongs to hand each of them a steaming sausage. Molly held her hot, greasy sausage gingerly and wondered what to do next.

"Now, what do you want on your sausage? Mustard? Relish? Kraut?" Uncle Dan asked.

"Why are we wearing these gloves?" Molly asked.

"So you don't burn your hands," Anton explained. "The sausages are very hot. Just remember to give me the gloves back after you are done. Some of the visitors are keeping the gloves as souvenirs. It's costing me a fortune!"

Molly nibbled the end of her sausage. "This is awkward," she observed. "Couldn't you just put it in a bun or something?"

"A bun?" Anton looked puzzled.

"Sure. Just slice open a bun and put the sausage in the middle. That way people can eat the sausage in the bun without burning their hands. You wouldn't need to worry about getting your gloves back, either." Molly frowned as she looked at her sausage.

"Let's try it. Henry!" Anton called. "Three buns, and slice them in half!"

"Not all the way through," Molly added.

"And don't slice them all the way through!" Anton shouted. Turning back to his three customers, Anton motioned for them to come back to the counter.

Soon Henry had three fresh buns sliced nearly in half and opened like a hinged lid. Anton took the sausages back and laid them in the buns. "Now, you try that, and tell me if you like it!"

Uncle Dan took a tentative bite and chewed it for a few seconds. A smile broke across his face. "It's delicious, Anton!"

"This is wonderful! I will serve all of my sausages this way from now on!" Anton was beaming.

"Paddy," Molly whispered. "Did I just invent the hot dog?"

"Possibly," he whispered back. "But I think Anton is going to get credit for it."

Paddy attacked his hot dog hungrily. Uncle Dan had to buy him another before he was satisfied. They washed their meal down with bottles of ice-cold root beer that Uncle Dan purchased from a nearby vendor. "Hires root beer, new at the Fair as well!" he laughed.

Refreshed, they walked further into the Midway. Paddy suddenly stopped and shouted, "Molly! Molly, do ye see what I'm seein'?" He pointed ahead of them.

Molly stared at the stone tower in front of them. "I see it, but I don't believe it." She turned to Uncle Dan. "That's Blarney Castle!"

"That it is, that it is!" Uncle Dan chuckled. "A visual treat for visitors to the Fair! Oh, it's not the real thing," he added as Paddy looked a bit concerned. "It's a recreation, sent as a gift from the people of Ireland."

"It's a pretty good recreation," Paddy murmured. "The color o' the stone is a bit off, but they got the shape right."

Past Blarney Castle they found the Irish Village on their right, where Donegal Castle had been recreated as well. "A good likeness," Paddy nodded. He whispered to Molly, "For this time, anyway. It was restored in the 1960s."

Uncle Dan had a grand time introducing Paddy to everyone in the Village. They all remarked on how much he looked like a real leprechaun, although Molly suspected that none of them had ever seen a leprechaun before. Paddy seemed to enjoy being the center of attention without worrying about someone trying to capture him.

Molly, on the other hand, started to get bored. "Uncle Dan," she whined, "Can we see the Ferris Wheel now? You promised!"

"Yes, yes of course! Let me say goodbye here and rescue our leprechaun from his newfound fame!" In a few minutes he returned with a jubilant looking Paddy.

"That was the best time I've ever had in me life!" he laughed.

"You played your part perfectly, my friend!" Uncle Dan chuckled. "It's as if you were born to be a leprechaun!"

"The Ferris Wheel?!" Molly fumed.

"Our next stop, my dear! Straight on down the Midway, and I guarantee you won't miss it!" Uncle Dan walked off down the street as Molly and Paddy struggled to keep up.

"Is something wrong, Molly?" Paddy asked.

"No, nothing that Mr. Popularity can fix," she grumbled.

"Oh, so *that's* it!" Paddy grinned. "I was the main attraction on Irish Day for an hour, and I shouldn't enjoy the moment?"

Molly was silent for a moment, and then she shook her head. "I'm sorry, Paddy. I guess I'm still worried about how to get home. Maybe I'll get an idea while I'm on the Ferris Wheel. There's a lot of time to think while they load and unload the cars."

Paddy looked up and gave a low whistle. "Is there anything this Fair *doesn't* have?"

Molly looked up and gasped. Right in the middle of the Midway sat a huge wheel. It had to be the tallest thing at the Exposition. The cars hanging from the wheel looked like small houses. For all of its size, the giant wheel turned easily with very little noise.

"Do you like it, Molly?" Uncle Dan shouted over the crowd. "There are thirty-six cars, each car holds sixty people! It stands 264 feet tall! Come with me, I have special pass privileges!"

They walked quickly to the front of the line. "We have a real leprechaun with us today! Happy Irish Day to you!" Uncle

Dan called as they boarded the third car. Each car had more than thirty seats, but there was plenty of room for passengers to walk around as well. The walls were made of a metal screen surrounded by glass, making the car feel secure while providing a wonderful view.

Six cars loaded at the same time. As their car moved up, up, up Molly felt her stomach jump. It was almost like being in an airplane, only the airplane hadn't been invented yet, she reminded herself. The wheel stopped again for the next six cars to unload and load. Finally their car was sitting at the top of the Ferris Wheel.

Uncle Dan explained how the Ferris Wheel turned. "Once all of the cars have taken on new passengers, we will make one complete revolution, and then start unloading. I took one of the first rides with Mrs. Ferris when the wheel opened."

Molly looked around, admiring the view. The White City lay gleaming in the afternoon sun. She turned to look the other way and felt her knees almost buckle. Paddy rushed to her side. "Molly, are ye all right? What is it?"

She closed her eyes and opened them again. "Paddy, we may be closer to home than we think."

"What do ye mean, girl?"

Molly raised her arm and pointed.

In the distance stood a tall, thin building, jet black against the horizon with two white shafts rising from its top. The afternoon sun glinted off its edges. It looked taller than even the Ferris Wheel.

"Molly, what is that building?" Paddy whispered.

Molly took in a shaky breath. "That is the Sears Tower. Paddy, that building is from *my* time. We have to get there."

chapter five

Through a Glass Darkly

Molly and Paddy raced through the streets of Chicago. "Molly, can ye slow down for a minute?" the leprechaun pleaded. He stopped to lean against a brick wall, bent over at the waist and holding his side.

The girl stopped as well, coming back to where Paddy gasped for air. "Paddy, we've got to hurry!" She paced nervously in a circle, clenching her fists in frustration. "I don't know how long the Sears Tower will be here!"

A wry smile broke through the pain on his face. "It ... still has a mortgage outstanding ... on it. It'll be here ... for a bit longer," he wheezed between ragged breaths.

Molly gave a short laugh. "How do you do it? How can you ... make jokes at a time like this? Whew, I'm short of breath, too. Maybe we *should* slow down a little bit." She lowered her head, taking deep breaths. "Or I could just carry you."

Paddy shook his head. "No, I'll not be carried about like a doll. Give me just a minute, and I'll be fine." He stood up, craning his neck back as he took in another long breath. "We left Uncle Dan in a big hurry. He seemed to take it pretty well, though." Paddy grinned. "It was grand being there on Irish Day, wasn't it?"

They resumed their journey at a brisk walk. The large building loomed above them, its twin white antennae unmistakable in the late afternoon sun.

"It's funny," Molly said, "I've lived in Chicago my whole life and I've never been to the Sears Tower right here in the city. It's the tallest building in the whole country!"

"I know what ye mean," Paddy agreed. "Four hundred years I've lived in Eire, and I've yet to visit Tara, the ancient capital city. The *Lia Fáil* sittin' right under me own nose, and I never get around to even look at one o' the four great treasures of Eire."

"The *Stone of Destiny?* What does it do?"

"It would roar out loud when the true king of Eire would put his feet on it. It did, anyway, until one king struck it with his sword when the stone didn't cry out for his hand-picked successor. By the way, ye did it again."

"Did what again?" Molly looked puzzled.

"Ye understood the Irish, just as I told ye last summer. I said the Irish name *Lia Fáil,* and ye knew right away that it meant the Stone o' Destiny."

Molly shook her head. "Paddy, you said *the Stone of Destiny,* not some Irish name. I told you, I don't understand Irish."

"We'll see about that when we have more time. I know what I said. Anyway, it looks like you're finally going to visit your Sears Tower. We're almost there!"

"We're not going to the Sears Tower, Paddy." Molly stopped, and the leprechaun turned and looked at her in disbelief.

"But I thought the whole reason for comin' here was because ye saw that Tower from the top o' the Ferris Wheel!"

"It is. But it's not the Sears Tower I was looking for." Molly turned and pointed at the glass building in front of them. "This is the building where my dad works. It's pretty close to the Sears Tower. I figured if the Sears Tower was here, my dad's building would be here, too."

"Seems like ye figured right. Do ye think he's here now?" Paddy walked to Molly's side.

"Only one way to find out. Ladies first!" Laughing, Molly raced for the revolving door. She had to keep the door spinning so that Paddy could follow in the next section, as he had never used one before.

Molly consulted the directory hanging in the lobby. "Yep, there's his office. Even if he's not here, we can call someone." Paddy surveyed the gleaming stainless steel lobby as they walked to the elevator. Molly found an empty car and ushered the elf inside.

She pushed the button marked '23' and the elevator doors closed. The elevator jerked slightly as it began its swift climb. "Don't be nervous, Paddy," Molly smiled. "The only thing safer than elevators is riding in an airplane."

The elevator chimed as its doors opened to the 23rd floor. Molly raced down the hallway to her father's suite. She flung the door open and burst into the room.

"Dad!" she shrieked. The red-haired man behind the computer screen looked up in surprise, and then smiled at the interruption.

"Oh, hi, honey. What are you doing here?" He then returned to his work.

"Dad?" Molly said uncertainly. She looked down at Paddy, who shrugged.

Molly walked over to the desk and leaned in close to the man sitting there. "Dad, it's me, Molly! I've been gone for almost a whole day, and I just found the way back! What are you doing that's so important?"

"Some other time, honey, I'm trying to get some work done." He frowned slightly as he began typing a memo.

"Molly, what's going on?" Paddy whispered. "He doesn't seem at all interested that there's a leprechaun standing in his office."

"He's only interested in his work," Molly whispered. "It's like it was before I went to Ireland, and before Mom got sick."

The door to the hallway opened behind them, and Molly turned to see who it was.

Sean O'Malley closed the door gently behind him and looked around. "Hey, sport, I'm glad you came to see me! Who's your friend?"

Molly looked at her father standing in the doorway, then she looked around at her father sitting behind the computer. She wavered for a moment before she collapsed onto the nearby sofa like a marionette whose strings had just been cut.

Paddy walked to the man in the doorway and extended his hand. "Paddy Finegan's the name! Are ye Mr. Sean O'Malley, then?"

"Why, yes I am! I'm pleased to meet you!" He looked over at Molly and his smile fled. "Molly, are you all right? You sat down rather suddenly!" He moved quickly to her side. "Can I get you a glass of water or something?"

Molly stared wide-eyed at the man next to her. She nodded.

"Paddy, can you get a glass of water for her? The cooler's right over there. I want to make sure she's all right." The second Mr. O'Malley sat down beside her. "Everything's going to be fine, sweetie. I'll take you straight home and we'll all have a nice family dinner together. Push the blue lever, Paddy."

Paddy returned with the water and handed it to Molly. She sipped it uncertainly, her eyes now shadowed with fear. She whispered, "Paddy, am I going crazy?"

The leprechaun folded his arms. "Actually, I think we're startin' to figure things out."

"What do you mean?" She took another sip of water.

Paddy sighed and climbed up onto the other end of the sofa. "Ye know the coin that I gave ye?"

"The one that caused all the trouble?"

"That's the one. I enchanted the coin to bring ye to me. *Specifically* to me."

"I don't see what you're getting at, Paddy."

"When ye put the coin into the pouch in that prison cell, ye had your arms wrapped around me. The coin was never intended to work with me! So, I figure the coin got — confused."

"The coin got confused?"

Paddy nodded. "Aye. That coin was not from the real world."

Molly felt like someone had hit her in the stomach. "Where was it from, then?"

"It's from the land o' *Fannléas*."

"The land of Glimmer?" Molly said softly. "What does that mean?"

"It means ye understand Irish, girl, but we'll figure that out later. I'll stick with English for now, then. The land o' Glimmer is a place where ideas are real. It's the place where all o' the fairy magic draws its power. When the coin got confused, instead o' bringing ye to the Chicago in the real world, it sort o' defaulted to bringing ye back to its native realm. It still brought ye to Chicago, but it was an ideal Chicago, the one o' the Exposition."

"And the Chicago of the Sears Tower." Molly thought about that for a minute. "The Sears Tower is also a symbol of what Chicago can be. Oh, you mean, ideas become ..." She gasped, turning to view the man at the computer. "That's not my real dad? That's just an idea that *looks* like Dad?"

Paddy nodded. "Let's call him Work-dad. The other one sittin' beside ye we'll call Family-dad. I'd say that both o' them are ideas that are still floatin' around."

Family-dad nodded. "Now Molly, you know I'll do anything for you and your mom. I took the job closer to home so I could spend more time with you."

Molly looked at Family-dad. "Well, what about *him?*" She indicated Work-dad with her head. "He's still here. He hasn't gone away. Doesn't that mean that my real dad still has that idea somewhere? Could he go back to being that way?"

She set the water down on the side table and stood up. "We're not in the real world yet, Paddy. And I know now that Dad is still struggling with the idea of working so hard that he could neglect Mom and me again. I can't let that idea win out. I've got to get back to the real world and help Dad before it's too late!"

"Aye, there are both good ideas and bad ideas. They all exist here in Glimmer." Paddy sighed again. "What do we do now?"

"Let's try to fix this." Molly knelt beside Paddy and put her arms around him. She held the leather pouch in one hand and pulled the golden coin out with the other.

Nothing happened.

"Molly, the coin won't work while you're in Glimmer. The enchantment is made to pull the power from Glimmer over to the real world!"

"We'll see about that! I want to go home *now!*" She pushed the coin back into the pouch.

Nothing happened.

"Molly, the coin won't work here, your silver bracelet won't work here, none o' the magic that was enchanted in the real world will work here!"

Molly sat down on the carpet. Tears slowly rolled down her cheeks. "Paddy, what are we going to *do?*"

"Do ye know why Eire is such a magical place? It's because Eire is closer to Glimmer than most other places in the real world. It's a place where the boundary between ideas and reality is thinner." He paused to rub his hands together.

"Ye crossed over the boundary into Glimmer from the real Eire once. Maybe we need to go to the Eire here in Glimmer, and cross back over to the real world from there!"

Molly blinked and wiped her eyes with her sleeve. "Maybe I've just been hanging around leprechauns too much, but that sort of makes sense. How do we get back to Ireland from here?"

Paddy yawned. "I guess on a boat. We can go back to the pier tomorrow morning and see what we can find. We need to get somethin' to eat and get some rest tonight, though."

"I have some sandwiches I made before I left home." She pulled them out of her backpack and opened the plastic bag. "Eeww! These smell nasty. I forgot, these have been in my backpack all day." She tossed the sandwiches into the trash bin.

"Now what do we do?" Paddy asked. "We don't have any food."

"I think I can handle that," Molly nodded. She walked into the office where Work-dad continued to type into his computer.

"Hey, Dad," Molly said sweetly. "I'm hungry. Can you give me some money for the vending machines?"

"Oh, sure, honey." He removed his wallet and handed her a twenty-dollar bill.

"I'm really hungry, Dad."

"Of course, dear, take another twenty. Will that be enough?"

Molly smiled broadly. "Oh, that's plenty. Thank you, Dad!" Work-dad was already engaged in his typing by the time she walked away.

Paddy looked at her in amazement. "Did you do that kind o' thing before?"

Molly fanned the money in her hand and made a theatrical curtsey. "He always would give Mom and me all the money we wanted. It used to make me mad, because what I really wanted …" she looked at Family-dad sitting on the sofa … "was his time, not his money. But it came in handy tonight. He's just an idea. I have to get back home and stop Work-dad there."

"It's ironic that you're using Work-dad here to get home and stop him there." Paddy grinned. "What's a vending machine?"

chapter six

The Galway Hooker

a hint of fall was in the air as Molly and Paddy approached the entrance to the Midway. Molly was glad she had her jacket to ward off the early morning chill.

"I hope the Fair is open this early," she said. "I don't know of any way to get back to the pier except to go back through the Exposition."

"This is the gate that we left from last night. There must be an entrance close by." Paddy looked around. "Ah, there's a sign! I didn't expect they would make it hard to find."

A young man was at the gate waiting for visitors to arrive. He greeted them with a yawn. "You folks are up early. Some of the exhibits won't be open for a couple of hours, but you're welcome to walk around. That'll be a dollar, please." He looked at Paddy and grinned. "Nice outfit. Too bad you weren't here yesterday. It was Irish Day. You would have been a hit!"

"Oh!" Molly gasped. "I forgot that there is an admission charge to get into the Fair! Paddy, our tickets were only good for one day! What are we going to do?"

Paddy's eyes twinkled. "I suppose I'll just have to dig into me vast fortune and buy a couple o' tickets." He emptied a small pouch onto the counter. Quarters, dimes, nickels and pennies clattered and bounced around as they formed an unruly pile of change. "Take what ye need, young fellow, I don't understand this American money."

Molly stared at the money in amazement. "Paddy, where did you get that?"

"If you'll recall, I was 'Mr. Popularity' as you put it, for a couple of hours yesterday. It seems that tourists here enjoy bein' entertained and they show their appreciation by fillin' the performer's hat. I even got one o' those Columbian half-dollars like Uncle Dan had!" He displayed the shiny coin with the Santa Maria, Columbus' flagship engraved on the back.

The attendant pinched out a dollar and Paddy swept the rest back into the pouch. Soon the girl and elf were walking through the Midway once again.

"Paddy, I'm sorry I yelled at you yesterday. It turned out to be pretty helpful for you to pretend to be a leprechaun and put on a show." Molly looked down at the leprechaun and tried to smile.

"Think nuttin' of it, dear girl," Paddy grinned. "It was worth it to see the look on your face when I dumped all o' those coins out!"

Within a short time they reached the Court of Honor. The White City loomed over them as they walked along the still waters of the Great Basin. "It's so hard to believe that none of this is real," Molly murmured as the golden Statue of the Republic grew larger.

"I didn't say this wasn't real. I said this wasn't the real world. Glimmer is a world where ideas *become* real. At least, while we're in Glimmer. It's important to the fairy folk, and apparently it's important to the human world as well." He waved his hand toward the gleaming white stucco buildings that surrounded them. "And don't forget Work-dad and Family-dad."

"I know," Molly sighed. "It's more than a dream, but it's not quite real to me yet. Not since I saw the Sears Tower, anyway, and certainly not since I found my dad — *twice!*"

They climbed the steps to the Peristyle and passed through the great arch. Lake Michigan stretched out before them, the sun dazzling on the water. Below them several ships were tied up to the pier where they had docked yesterday.

Paddy gave a low whistle. "I think I've found our boat."

"How can you be sure? We just got here!"

"If we're goin' to Eire, we need an Irish boat. And *that* is an Irish boat!" He pointed to a dark-hulled sailboat bobbing gently by the pier.

The boat was about thirty feet long, with a black hull. A single mast held a dark rust-brown mainsail, and two smaller triangle shaped sails of the same color hung toward the front of the boat. The name *Leela* was painted carefully in white letters across the bow.

"What kind of Irish boat is it?"

"It's a hooker ship from Galway. They were invented to handle the tricky winds and currents o' Galway Bay. That one there is a *Gleoiteog* type, used for fishing and cargo. They're not found anywhere else in the world." Paddy smiled as he admired the beautiful lines of the sails.

"Well, we found one here in Chicago." Molly was skeptical. "Do you think it's here because we were thinking about going to Ireland?"

Paddy considered that for a moment. "It's possible, though I wasn't thinking of a hooker ship to get us back. Maybe we should ask the captain why he's here?"

A man stepped from the small cabin on the hooker and stood up, his tweed cap pulled low over jet-black hair flecked with grey. His leather vest showed wear from salt-spray and sunlight. He climbed to the dock and began untying a line.

"We'd best hurry, Molly, it looks like he's gettin' ready to cast off!"

The two rushed down the remaining steps to the pier and over to the hooker where they paused, gasping for breath. The captain wheeled to look at them.

His eyes widened when he saw Paddy. "Now *you're* a long way from home, lad, that's for sure!"

"Aye, and further than ye know!" Paddy responded, taking another deep breath. "Are ye returning to Eire directly?"

"Ya," the captain answered. "Is it the two of ye, then?" Molly nodded.

"How will ye be payin' your fare?" He looked at Molly and Paddy.

"Paddy, would you mind ..." Molly began.

"Who, me?" Paddy asked with a surprised look. "I'm just a poor traveler, stranded halfway around the world without a penny to me name. It's a trial being so poor, I just try not to burden me friends ..."

"It's all right, Paddy," Molly sighed. "It's not real money, anyway."

The captain raised his eyebrow. "Not real money? You're trying to cheat me, ye are?"

"Oh, pay no attention to the child, she doesn't know what she's sayin'. O' course me money's real, what little there is of it, trust Paddy Finegan on that. I was savin' it for me poor family in Eire ..." Paddy pulled out his small pouch and shook some coins into his hand.

"First ye have no money, now ye have money but a poor family has appeared back home! You're not foolin' Michael O'Flaherty, sir, you're a leprechaun or I'm not a fisherman! I've no use for American money, anyway, real or not." The captain scowled and turned again to free the line.

Molly's face brightened. "I have something real, Captain O'Flaherty!" She pulled an apple from her backpack. "This apple is as real as it gets. Try a bite, if you don't believe me."

He looked uncertainly at the red fruit before plucking it from Molly's outstretched hand. "Smells all right," he muttered, and he took a big bite. A smile grew on his face as he chewed, a trickle of sweet juice running down into his beard. "Now *this* is an apple! I've not tasted anything so grand in me life!"

He bowed stiffly and pointed to the boat. "Your passage is paid, me lady." Scowling at Paddy, he added, "And ye can bring the liar along too, if ye want."

"Thank you, Captain! We'll try not to be any trouble." Molly smiled as she stepped into the boat. Paddy growled a harrumph, straightened his hat and jumped nimbly into the boat after her.

Within minutes the *Leela* was free of the dock and headed away from the pier. Captain O'Flaherty adjusted the foresails to catch the breeze and send the boat skipping through the water. Molly looked ahead to the eastern horizon, where the sun was climbing higher in the sky.

"I've been to Lake Michigan lots of times, and it's never smelled this good before," she said. "There's no dead fish or anything."

"Remember where we are, Molly," Paddy said in a low voice as he looked to the back of the boat where the captain held the tiller. "Glimmer is a place where all o' the best ideas can be real. But I have to warn ye."

"Warn me about what?" Molly questioned, turning to him.

"I told ye that ideas can be both good and bad. It's like dreams; ye can have a pleasant dream, or ye can have a nightmare. They're both dreams, but they are very different."

Molly shuddered at the thought. "I used to have nightmares before Dad decided to cut back on his work and spend more time with Mom and me. They were awful." She looked out to the horizon again. "Are you saying we can find a nightmare here in Glimmer, and it can be *real?*"

Paddy nodded somberly. "Finding your Work-dad here may have only been a first taste of a nightmare."

Molly shook her head. "I hope not. I need to get back before anything else happens. Speaking of getting back, I have a question for the captain." She walked to the back of the swaying boat.

"Excuse me, Captain O'Flaherty, but are you planning on using the St. Lawrence Seaway to get to Ireland?"

"Do I plan on using the *what?*" he replied.

"The St. Lawrence Seaway."

"Why would I use that?"

"To get around Niagara Falls. Niagara Falls connects Lake Ontario to Lake Erie, but it drops about a hundred and seventy feet."

The captain grinned. "Well, if ye wanted to see the Falls, why didn't ye just say so?" He pulled hard on the tiller and the little ship turned toward a fog bank.

"What are you doing?" Molly shrieked. "You're going right into that mist! You won't be able to see!"

The *Leela* had already slipped into the billowing mist. Molly could see nothing as the boat lurched on the choppy water. "It won't be long now!" shouted the captain. Molly realized he was shouting because a dull roaring noise was getting louder and louder.

"Take us out! Take us out! You're going to get us all killed!" Molly rushed to the captain and began beating her fists on his shoulder. "Go back!"

"All right, have a seat before ye fall overboard," Captain O'Flaherty chuckled. He tugged on the tiller again and the boat bounced away from the roar. Molly put her arm up to protect herself from the spray, but she was getting soaked.

Suddenly the mist lifted. The boat bobbed on the turbulent water. Molly looked up and could not believe what she saw.

High above her, surrounding the boat on three sides, a huge horseshoe shaped waterfall poured down. The roar was deafening, but they were moving away from it now.

Paddy tugged at her sleeve. He too was soaked. Paddy shouted, "What is it, Molly? Do ye know where we are?"

Molly nodded. "This is Niagara Falls — from the bottom side!" she shouted back. "How did we get here so fast? How did we get around the Falls?"

The brave little boat moved away from the mist, its rust-brown sails glistening with moisture. Now another set of falls drew closer on their starboard side, falling in a straight line instead of a great curve.

"Those are the American Falls — the horseshoe falls are on the Canadian side! My mother and I came to Niagara last year!" She turned to the captain, who had water running off of his cap. "What are we doing here?"

"You're the one who suggested this, and a fine suggestion it was. But we'd best finish this, seein' as we're soaking wet already ..." with that the captain turned the boat back toward the mist.

"What are you doing?" Molly screamed.

Paddy grabbed her hand firmly and tugged. "Come with me, Molly!" he shouted over the roar of the falls. Pulling her to the deck, he jerked an oilskin tarp over them.

They could hear the thunder of the water, and now the spray hitting the tarp like a child beating a drum. The boat pitched violently in the waves as they huddled together.

Strangely, the noise from the falls seemed to get softer, and the pitter-patter of water on the tarp slowed and then stopped altogether. The boat rocked up and down, but gently, like a baby in its mother's arms.

Molly peeked out from under the tarp. Captain O'Flaherty sat by the tiller, looking out over the sea. They *were* on the sea, with no land in sight, and the roar of the mighty falls was gone. Only the lapping of the swells against the prow could be heard, and sails flapping in the salty breeze.

Molly threw the tarp back and marched over to the captain. "Why did you do that, and … where are we, anyway?" She stood with her hands propped on her hips.

The captain smiled at the red-haired girl waiting for his answer. "It's faster goin' through the mist, but it is a rougher trip, I'll grant ye that." He removed his leather vest, still wet from the spray, and set it beside him to dry. "Ye can't tell if you're goin' into or comin' out of a mist, but a mist is a mist. If ye have a clear idea o' where ye want to come out, ye can cut out most o' the travel in between. Right now we're somewhere in the North Atlantic, headin' for Eire. Do ye have a particular port you're going to, or do ye expect me to invite ye home for dinner?"

Paddy brushed water from his sleeve. "Can ye find Donegal without goin' through another mist?" He removed his own green jacket and shook the water off of it.

"Sure, and do ye know where in that fair land ye wish to go?"

"As close to O'Doherty's keep at Buncrana as ye can. We'll find our way from there."

Molly looked at Paddy with concern. "Paddy," she whispered, "won't you be in trouble if you go to Donegal? Isn't that where the Fairy Queen lives?"

"Aye," he whispered back, "and there's no greater concentration o' magic anywhere in the world. If there's any place in Glimmer where we can get back to the real world, it's there."

"But aren't you still wanted for taking the coin?" she persisted.

The elf nodded glumly. "I have to take that chance. I might be able to survive here in Glimmer, but your home is on the other side."

Molly hugged the little man. "I couldn't bear to lose you!"

"Everything all right, there?" the captain asked.

"We're fine," Molly gulped, and brushed back a tear. "We've just been traveling a lot recently, and we're not through yet."

"Speakin' o' traveling, how is it ye were in Chicago with this fine boat?" Paddy asked.

"Ah, that," the captain murmured. His eyes focused softly on the horizon. "I was lookin' for me wife."

chapter seven

The Tale of the Merrow

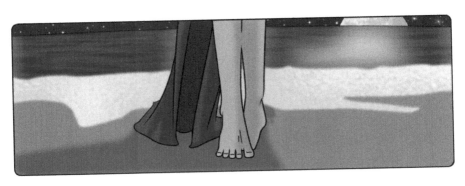

*Y*our wife?" Molly asked. "You don't know where your wife is?"

Captain O'Flaherty shook his head sadly. "It's a long story. I don't want to bore ye."

"We've a few hours at least to reach Eire, don't we? I've not known the Irish to be shy of either tellin' stories or hearin' them." Paddy grinned as he found a seat.

"It's probably a sad story, Paddy," Molly said. But she sat down beside Paddy and crossed her legs under her. "Maybe it would help if you talked about it. I know it helps me sort things out."

"Well, it would help pass the time," the captain agreed. He checked his compass and adjusted the tiller, and then he settled into a comfortable position and began his story.

"I remember the day I met Leela like it was yesterday," the captain said dreamily as he pulled on the tiller. "The fishing was no good that day, and I came in to the dock early. I decided to take the long way home along the beach to let my temper cool down.

"When I reached the rocks I saw something odd. Behind one o' the boulders was a grey fur cloak, like seal skin.

It looked like someone was trying to hide it, and not doing a very good job of it. I took it with me, thinkin' I could make something o' the day.

"Later that night I had just cleared the table after supper, when there was a knock at the door. I opened it to find a beautiful young woman shivering on me doorstep. Her hair was the color o' golden flax, her lips almost blue. Her eyes were like blue ice, or gemstones polished to a fine luster. She was wrapped only in an old sheet, apparently borrowed from someone's clothesline."

"What had happened to her?" Molly asked.

"I noticed her hand as she held the sheet around her," the captain continued. "Her fingers had the most delicate webbing between them. I had not believed the legends to be true, but here she was on my very own doorstep."

"What legends?" Molly wondered out loud.

"The legends o' the merrows, the fairy folk who live under the sea. The females are said to be quite beautiful. This one certainly was. They can only come ashore in human form if they take off their cloak and leave it behind."

"So a merrow is a mermaid?"

"Ye might think of her as an Irish mermaid. She asked me, 'Please, kind sir, I've lost me cloak and cannot find where I've laid it. Can ye help me find it? I need it very badly.'

" 'What is your name?' I asked her.

" 'Leela,' she replied.

" 'Sure, and it's I that have your cloak, dear lady,' I says. 'Come into me house.' "

The captain stopped to look out over the ocean for a moment. His voice was thick when he continued. "I'm not proud o' what happened next. I told her that she must marry me, for she couldn't return to the sea without her cloak. She pleaded and cried and begged me to give her cloak back. My heart must o' been stone. Finally she agreed, and Father O'Flannigan married us at the parish.

"I was very happy for many years. Leela was beautiful and caring. She worked hard to keep the house in proper order. We had no lack o' money, for she would go to the seashore and ask her sisters to bring her gold and treasure salvaged from sunken ships.

"We had three children; Sean, Brigid, and James. You'll not find a better mother than me dear Leela. The children adored her, o' course.

"One day I found her crying in the kitchen. I asked her what was the trouble.

" 'Oh, Michael, ye know what the trouble is,' she said. 'You've taken my cloak, and I can't return to my family. I miss them so!' and she burst into tears again."

Molly nodded. "I miss my family already, and I've only been gone two days. Leela must have felt terrible."

Michael continued. "I must have learned to love her through the years, for me heart nearly broke at seein' her misery. I turned on me heel and walked straight to the hiding place to get the cloak. When I came back to the kitchen, I pressed the bundle into her webbed fingers and said, 'There, there, Leela, I'll not be causing ye any more pain. Freely I return your cloak, and ask your forgiveness for a poor Irishman smitten with your beauty.'

"We walked to Galway Bay together, she clutching the cloak and looking at me as though I was going to snatch it back. At the water's edge she slipped out of her dress and pulled the cloak around her. As it came over her head, she looked just like a seal, with fur as grey as a thunderstorm over Connemara. She looked up at me with those eyes like blue ice, and slid into the waves."

He paused to wipe a tear from his bristled cheeks. "That's the last time I saw my Leela. I named me boat *Leela*, and I've been sailin' the oceans looking for her ever since. The children were angry with me when I told them what I'd done, how I had trapped their mother against her will. James was only fourteen and blamed me for letting her go at first. Now they all feel sorry for me, seeing how much I grieve for their mother and travel the world hoping for a glimpse of her."

They were silent for a few minutes as the boat ploughed through the waves. A gull circled overhead, its raspy cry causing Molly to look up.

"How far do gulls travel from shore?" she asked.

"That one, not too far. Take a look from the top o' the next swell."

As the *Leela* crested the next wave, Molly saw land peeking above the horizon. "Is that Ireland?" she asked excitedly.

"Donegal. The home o' the good people."

"The good people?" Molly asked, wrinkling her brow.

"He means the fairy folk," Paddy answered. "Many o' the humans refer to us as the 'good people' for fear of insulting us." He glared at the captain, who merely snorted in reply. "O' course, someone who's mistreated a merrow for most of his life probably thinks nuttin' of insulting a leprechaun."

"Paddy, that's not nice," Molly scolded. "You *were* lying about having a family and not having money, and I think Captain O'Flaherty is suffering right now. I think he really loves Leela." Her eyes widened as she looked over Paddy's head. "Ooh, what is that?"

The others turned to follow her gaze. The captain was the first the react. He leaped to his feet and rushed to the side of the boat. Molly feared he would fall right over the side.

Bobbing in the waves twenty yards away was a small object. Although she had never seen one in the wild before, Molly felt sure it was a seal. It looked dark grey in the water.

"Leela!" the captain roared. "Is it truly you, dear?"

The seal rolled over on its side and started to swim away. Swearing, the captain rushed to the tiller and swung the trim ship to follow.

The seal and the hooker ship made their way toward the distant shore. Although the seal could have dived beneath the waves and vanished, it did not do so. The captain adjusted the mainsail to keep their speed up as he pursued the seal.

After a couple of hours a small island no more than a few meters across showed up along their port side. The seal changed course and climbed on top of the rocks.

"Look, it is a seal!" Molly cried. "Are there any others?"

Captain O'Flaherty dropped the sails, bringing the ship to a stop just off the tiny island. The *Leela* bobbed gently in the waves. "Leela! Leela, is that you?" he cried frantically.

In response the seal raised its flippers to its head. The skin fell away to its shoulders, revealing golden hair that sparkled in the sun, then the head of a beautiful woman. Her ice blue eyes could be seen even from this distance.

"Michael," she called across the water. "You've pursued me these past years. What is it ye want, my love?"

"Leela! Oh, my darling Leela! It's your forgiveness I seek for all the harm I've done ye. The children send their love, we all miss ye so!"

"Michael, me darling, ye had my forgiveness the day you gave the cloak back. There's not many Irishmen would do that. Your heart's not as cold as ye think, for ye truly loved me. And when you released me, I realized that I truly loved you."

"Then come back to us, Leela! Ye can go back to the sea whenever ye want! Will ye come back, dear?"

"No, Michael O'Flaherty, I won't come back to ye. I'd have to take off me cloak again, and there's no tellin' that a person with a heart as good as yours will be the one who finds it. I've spent me days on the land, and I'll stay the rest o' them in the sea."

The captain wept bitterly at this, and Molly came close to lay her hand on his shoulder in comfort. "Bless ye, child," he managed, "but there'll be nothing ye can do for this old fisherman."

"One thing I'll do for ye, Michael," Leela called again. The captain looked up hopefully. "I'll stay close to the shore where I can see you and the children. But I'll not take off me cloak again."

"Thank you, Leela, me darling!"

"Where are ye going, Michael?"

"I'm taking these two to Donegal, down Inishowen way."

"There are dangerous shoals between here and Donegal. I'll lead you safe through them if you'll follow me." Leela pulled the cloak over her head, and once more nothing other than a grey seal appeared to be sitting on the rocks.

"I'll follow you anywhere!" he cried, and jumped to raise the sails again. The merrow slid into the water and swam ahead of them toward the shore. Time and again she led her namesake around the dangerous rocks that lurked beneath the water. Always the captain kept his shining eyes on the dark grey shape that bobbed and leaped in the water ahead of the little hooker ship.

At last the coast of Donegal came clearly into view. Sharp fingers of rock stabbed into the ocean, and shallow bays led to a sandy beach between cliffs of marvelous beauty. Lush green grass covered the hillsides, and Molly thought she had never seen anything so beautiful and dangerous in her life. She felt a chill run up her spine just thinking about it.

The boat slid onto the beach with a smooth crunching noise. "I'll float her off on the high tide," the captain said. "You should be able to go ashore here safely. The keep is right there." He pointed to the stone walls that seemed to grow from the ridge above them.

"Thank you, Captain O'Flaherty. You don't know how much you've helped us." Molly gave the gruff fisherman a big smile.

The captain nodded. "Thank you for spotting Leela, Molly. Things will be getting back to normal now." He turned to look at the grey seal swimming just offshore. "Though I don't think anything is quite normal when you're married to a merrow.

"Take care o' that lying leprechaun. We need more of his kind with big hearts." When Paddy looked surprised the captain added, "I saw ye pull the girl under the tarp when we went back into the mist. I nearly fell overboard seeing a leprechaun help someone else! My compliments and blessings upon ye, Paddy Finegan o' the good people."

Paddy bowed slightly. "Perhaps I judged ye too quickly, Michael O'Flaherty," he smiled. "Time will tell."

They climbed to the beach and waved back to the captain as he stood on his ship's deck. Turning, they began the climb from the sand into the surrounding hills.

"Where do we go from here, Paddy?" Molly asked.

"From here we go to the castle o' the Fairy Queen," he said heavily. "Castle Tiarnach, deep in the heart o' Donegal."

chapter eight

The Build-a-Leprechaun Store

olly sat against the sprawling oak tree munching an energy bar. Paddy leaned back next to her, unwrapping his third candy bar. "Paddy," Molly said, "don't you think that's enough candy for now? We need to save some for later."

The leprechaun savored a small bite and closed his eyes. "Ah, Molly, this stuff is heaven. What did ye say it was again?"

"It's a 100 Grand bar," she sighed. "I'm glad you like it, but you're not used to eating all of this junk food. I'm worried how it might affect you."

"Don' worphy abouf me," he replied with his mouth full. "Theze are so chewy!"

"It's the caramel that makes them chewy. Here, have some water. I think you like them because they are named after money. They used to be called $100,000 bars, Mom told me once, after some TV game show."

Paddy nodded and took a sip of bottled water. "Oh, that's a grand treat!" he exclaimed. "I could eat these candy bars all day!"

Molly stood up and began stuffing the remainders of their snack into her backpack. "No, you couldn't, because we would run out of them. We've been walking since Captain

O'Flaherty dropped us off on the beach yesterday. We need to go easy on our food, or we'll run out of everything. I haven't seen another vending machine for a long time. How far do you think this castle is?"

"Probably another day's walk, I'd say." Paddy tried to balance the rest of his candy bar on the end of his nose.

"Paddy, what are you doing?"

The elf put the last bite of his candy bar on the top of his hat. "Look, now me hat's truly grand! In fact, it's 100 grand!" He laughed hysterically.

"Okay, I think two candy bars are your limit from now on," Molly said firmly. She grabbed the candy from the top of his hat and wrapped it in a plastic bag before dropping it into her backpack.

"Molly, that was mine!" Paddy protested.

"And it will be yours again tomorrow, when I hope this chocolate overdose has worn off. Let's start walking and burn off some of that energy."

Grumbling, the little man put his jacket back on and led the way into the forest. Spruce trees towered over them, and the sun made wonderful patterns as it searched out a path through the branches.

"Paddy," Molly said after a bit, "Do you remember when you told me that I could understand Irish?"

"O' course I do! You've proved it several times, now!"

"Then why didn't I know what a *cathair* was when we first met?"

Paddy stopped and looked at her. "Faith, you're right. Ye didn't know that a *cathair* is a stone ringfort. I had to tell ye, I did."

Molly nodded. "I've been thinking about that. You said that I knew Irish because I understood everything that Nefra said, and she always spoke in Irish. Except for the dragon talk, no one except Stanley could understand that."

"Aye, that's a fact."

"Maybe my ability to understand Irish has something to do with Nefra instead of something to do with me."

"Nefra? How could a black dragon have anything to do with this? What could Nefra have given you ..." his words trailed off as understanding washed over his face.

"Yes, what could Nefra have given me?" Molly smiled and pulled out her golden chain that held the stone medallion. "I've been wearing this or holding this ever since Nefra gave it to me before she left."

"But ye understood Nefra before she gave it to you! That doesn't explain it, Molly."

Molly slipped the chain over her head. She laid the necklace on a rock and stepped away. "Let's try an experiment. Say something in Irish to me, Paddy!"

Paddy shook his head. "All right. *Ta tuirse orm.*"

"Wow. 'Taw TEER-sheh urm.' That's Irish, all right. I have no idea what you just said." She sighed, relieved. "Now for the second part of the experiment. Pick up the medallion, Paddy, and try saying that again."

He picked up the carved stone medallion. *"Ta tuirse orm."*

"I don't care if you are tired, Paddy ... Oh, boy!" Molly put her hands to her head.

"What is it, Molly?"

Molly rubbed her temples gently. "I just heard your voice inside my head, almost like you were thinking the words to me. That hasn't happened to me since ..." She looked at the leprechaun. "Since I met Nefra. Paddy, every time Nefra said anything, I heard her voice inside my head. I think that her medallion translates Irish into English or something."

"And the thing translates it whether you're hearin' it or speakin' it?"

Molly nodded. "When Nefra gave me the medallion, I thanked her, and she told me I was welcome. I didn't hear her voice inside my head then, I just understood her plain as day."

"So when you have the medallion, ye understand the Irish without the speaker's voice being inside your head. But when I have the medallion, and I speak Irish, ye hear my voice inside your head." He handed the medallion back to Molly. "That explains how ye can understand Irish. Best ye be keeping this trinket around your neck. It could come in handy."

They resumed their trek into the forest. The tall spruce trees gave way to cypress trees, their trunks thick with age. Dark shadows covered the forest floor in the early afternoon.

Something off to the side caught Molly's eye. "Paddy, wait up a second. What is that?" She pointed into the woods. "There's a light flashing there. It's flashing really steady. That can't be natural, can it?"

Paddy stared at the light blinking through the trees. "I don't know, Molly. Shall we see what it is, then?"

"Whatever it is, it's green." Molly walked through the underbrush, being careful not to snag her clothes on the holly that grew in abundance. "It reminds me of those neon lights you see downtown, the ones that spell out … words …"

She stopped with her mouth wide open. A low building made of stones sat in a small clearing. It was much longer than a regular house, perhaps two hundred feet long. Grey smoke curled lazily from stone chimneys set in each end. Perched on top of the thatched roof was a large sign made with green neon lights that flashed the words:

Build-a-Leprechaun

"Paddy," she said uncertainly, "tell me you're seeing what I'm seeing."

"Aye," he confirmed, "though I've no explanation for it."

They walked slowly up to the front door. It was about four feet high, made of wood with metal bands to hold the boards together. An iron ring attached to the door appeared to serve as a knocker. A sign next to the door read:

All Visitors Must Obey the Rules
1. No Drinking the Whiskey Inside
2. No Taking the Whiskey Outside
3. All Sprouts Must be Reported for Monitoring

"That's interesting," Molly whispered. "Shall we knock?"

"Actually, I've always wondered where leprechauns came from meself," Paddy nodded.

Molly grasped the heavy iron ring and rapped it on the doorplate a couple of times. The noise echoed on the other side, then faded away. She reached for it again but stopped when she heard the thump-thump of running feet.

"I'm coming, I'm coming," wheezed a voice from inside. There was the sound of a metal bar sliding back, and the door swung inward to reveal a stocky leprechaun wearing a tunic and rust-red leggings. His beard was red and turning grey, while his eyebrows were black and bushy on his wrinkled face.

"Do ye have an appointment, then?" the old leprechaun demanded.

"Um, no, I'm afraid we don't," Molly said, looking at Paddy, who shrugged.

"Well, lucky for you we're not busy right now. Come on in." He shoved the door all the way open and motioned for them to enter.

Molly ducked low to get through the door, but inside the high ceiling of the thatched roof allowed her to stand comfortably. Paddy followed as their host closed the door and bolted it again.

"Name's Brian MacGinty. I'm the caretaker here," the leprechaun said. "Who are you?"

"Paddy Finegan," said Paddy cheerily.

"Molly O'Malley," Molly said with a slight bow.

Brian looked at Molly and squinted. "You're not a leprechaun. What sort o' fairy are ye?"

"A — a big one," Molly improvised.

Brian nodded. "Well, we don't build big ones here. We specialize in leprechauns. There're not many who know where leprechauns come from. Well, follow me."

He led the way down the hallway to a white door. Long rows of shelves filled with bottles stretched down the hall. Brian handed one bottle to Molly, and another bottle to Paddy. The handmade labels read 'Premium Irish Whiskey'.

"You've read the rules by the door outside, I reckon?" he asked, peering first at Molly and then Paddy.

"Well, yes, but they didn't make much sense." Molly looked at the bottle, puzzled. "This is Irish whiskey, and we're not supposed to drink it, or take it outside, but I don't know what we're supposed to do with it."

Brian sighed and shook his head. "Come with me, and I'll explain it to ye." He opened the white door and led them into the next room. It was a very large room that seemed to cover acres of ground. Bright lights hung from the ceiling, making everything as light as day. Narrow cobblestone paths snaked through the room, but elsewhere every square inch of ground was covered in lush clover.

"Now," the caretaker said, "First ye need to find a four-leaf clover. Don't pick it, whatever ye do."

"We have to find a four-leaf clover in all of that?" Molly asked in amazement.

"Only if ye want to build a leprechaun. Once ye find the four-leaf clover, pour one drop and one drop only of Irish whiskey on it."

"What happens if ye use more than one drop o' whiskey?" Paddy asked.

"Then you'll get a clurichaun. He'll be good for nuttin' and be thirstin' for more whiskey from then on. Just use one drop, then mark the spot with a stick to let me know where ye found it. Then report back." Brian turned to leave.

"That's how you build a leprechaun?" Molly murmured. "You just pour a drop of whiskey on a four-leaf clover and it makes a leprechaun?"

"Well, our clover is specially grown for this purpose. You'd just be pourin' your fine whiskey onto the ground if ye tried it anywhere else. That's why *we're* the Build-a-Leprechaun store."

"Do you sell franchises?" Paddy asked.

Brian smirked. "No, there's not much need for more stores. We only build leprechauns when we can find a four-leaf clover, so new leprechauns are rare to start with. Leprechauns live a long time, as you well know, Paddy, so there's little reason to replace the ones we already have, either."

"Well, *I* want to build a leprechaun!" Molly skipped down the cobblestones and began looking for four-leaf clovers. Paddy sighed and joined her.

Several hours later Paddy stood up and rubbed his back. "Oww, that hurts to bend over that long. Any luck yet, Molly?"

Molly shook her head. "My eyes are going all blurry looking at this clover. I'm not sure I could see a four-leaf clover if I was looking right at it. Like this one here … *oh!*"

"What is it, Molly, did ye find one?"

Molly nodded. "I think so. Take a look for yourself."

There in the clover field was a perfectly formed four-leaf clover. Since all of the other clovers had three leaves it was difficult to see, especially when they tended to overlap each other.

"I'm going to pour the drop of whiskey on it now, Paddy. Cross your fingers." Molly opened the whiskey bottle gently and lined up the mouth over the target. Slowly she tipped the bottle more and more until a single drop of whiskey dripped out and landed right in the middle of the four-leaf clover.

Molly carefully put the cap back on the whiskey and breathed a sigh of relief. "Boy, I'm glad I didn't make a clurichaun. Let's mark this spot and go find Brian."

Brian was amazed that they had found a four-leaf clover so quickly. "Ye certainly had the luck o' the Irish with ye today," he nodded. "It looks like a fine pour. The sprout should be up in a few weeks."

"What happens then?" Molly asked.

"We have another place in the back where the young leprechauns live for about forty years. We teach them all about shoemaking, everything they need to be fine cobblers."

"I think I remember this place now," Paddy said dreamily. "I was very young, but I liked learning how to make shoes."

"We cast an enchantment on our leprechauns when they leave, so that they forget the store. If they should find their way back again, as you did, it's not uncommon for some o' those memories to come back."

"Can I name my leprechaun?" Molly asked.

"I suppose," Brian said. "What name would ye have for him?"

"My favorite leprechaun name," she looked at Paddy with a grin, "is already taken. Let's go with Eric."

"Eric it is, then. Leprechauns generally take their last names from the owners o' land where they eventually settle. We'll leave that to Eric after he's grown."

Molly yawned. "It's getting dark out, isn't it? It must be nearly evening. Do you have a place where we can spend the night? Then we can be on our way in the morning." She looked at Paddy. "I think I got carried away building my leprechaun — Eric, I mean. We need to find our way back home."

Brian grinned. "We do have guest rooms for our visitors. But first I'd welcome your company at dinner with me tonight! We don't get that many folks passing through."

"That sounds grand!" Paddy exclaimed. "What do ye think, Molly?"

"I think it sounds great!" she smiled. "As long as we don't have any 100 Grand bars!"

chapter nine

Fionn

ionn stooped to pick up another piece of wood. Standing up again, he paused to admire the late orchid growing nearby, pink and white against the green moss.

It had been a change of pace, to say the least. Ever since he had come to live with the druid Finegas, things had been so different. These past two months had been almost a dream.

He brushed his blond hair out of his eyes as he looked toward the ancient arch standing in the clearing. No one knew where it came from, and it was rumored to be cursed. Fionn's finely-chiseled features frowned slightly, and he decided to give it a wide berth.

Suddenly a crackling like dry autumn leaves sounded across the field and yellow-orange lights flashed. The smell of sulfur hung in the air as all became still once more.

Then Fionn saw a girl step through the arch.

She had not been there a moment ago. Here she was, though, about his age or a little younger than his thirteen years. She had red hair, and her green eyes blinked as she looked around. Her clothes were strange, and he could not recall ever seeing a girl wear trousers before. She had a pack slung over her shoulders, and it too seemed out of place, as if made from some otherworldly material.

Fionn set the wood down as quietly as he could. "I'd better check this out," he muttered. "Master Finegas will be curious as well."

He stepped out into the clearing, walking toward the girl. As she saw him, her mouth shaped an "Oh!" He stopped and waved.

"Hello," he called in greeting. "Can I help you?"

"I didn't know anyone was here," the girl replied. "Paddy and I were just passing through, and … now where did that leprechaun get to?" She began looking around, seeming somewhat annoyed.

"Perhaps I can help you find your friend. Did you say a leprechaun? Is he just small then, or …?"

"No, he's a real leprechaun." She turned to Fionn and waved a stern finger at him. "And you'll treat him with the utmost respect or you'll answer to me!"

"And who are you?" Fionn responded with a twinkle in his eye.

"I'm Molly O'Malley, and I've seen things much scarier than you!" As she looked at him, she added to herself, *although I've not seen many that are better-looking*.

"My name's Fionn," the boy laughed, bowing slightly from the waist, "and I'll keep that in mind. Now, what does this friend of yours look like?"

"He's about two feet tall, wearing a green suit and a green top hat. He has black hair and blue eyes, no beard or mustache." Molly sighed. "If there's trouble anywhere around, that's probably where you'll find him."

"Well, there's no lack of trouble around here," Fionn frowned. "I've been lucky enough to meet my master, the druid Finegas. He is kind to me, and treats me more like a son than a servant."

"Where's your family?" Molly asked, looking behind an ash tree.

"A couple of days journey away. I hope they've forgotten me by now." Molly looked surprised at this, and he continued. "I have always been considered an evil omen in my family. My earliest memories are of being beaten and never having enough to eat."

"Why would your own family treat you like that?" Molly's eyes brimmed with tears.

"Because of this." He pulled back his long blond hair from his ears.

"Your ears — they're pointed!" Molly exclaimed. "Just like Paddy's!"

"So you think I might be a leprechaun, too?" Fionn grinned.

"No, probably not a leprechaun, but one of the fairy folk, maybe. If we were in the real world, you could pass for a Trekkie. You'd make an awesome Vulcan."

"I don't understand this 'Trekkie' word. Now 'Vulcan' is the Roman god of the forge, who makes the thunderbolts for Jupiter." He looked puzzled. "What do you mean by saying 'If we were in the real world?'"

"Paddy and I have been in Glimmer ever since I used the coin. We were hoping that Ireland was close enough to both worlds that we could cross over and return to the real world." Now Molly frowned. "You mean to say that this isn't Glimmer?"

"This is the real world as far as I know." Fionn shook his head. "Glimmer sounds like something in a fairy tale."

"Well, you look like you just stepped out of a fairy tale. Still, if this *could* be the real world …"

"I saw you come through the arch. It made strange noises and flashed bright colored lights. You weren't there before. I know because I was looking right at it."

"Hmmm …" Molly thought. "None of our magic seems to work in Glimmer. Which means, if this *is* the real world …"

She pulled up her sleeve and tapped her silver bracelet. "Paddy, come and find me. I hope this works across fairy dimensions."

"What are you doing?" Fionn asked as he came closer.

"Paddy gave me this bracelet. He enchanted it so when I rub it or tap it, he knows where I'm at. Then he can come and find me." She continued to tap the bracelet. "It's much easier than me trying to find a leprechaun."

A sound like the crackling of dry leaves sprang from the arch. Colors flashed wildly, and the smell of sulfur spread across the meadow. Then all became quiet, and Paddy stepped through the arch.

"Paddy!" Molly screamed, and she rushed to hug him. "I couldn't find you anywhere!"

"It was the strangest thing," Paddy mumbled as he returned the hug. "Ye disappeared while I was looking around the side o' the ruins. I called and called your name, but ye didn't answer. Then I felt the bracelet's charm and followed it through that arch. How did ye do that, girl? I thought the bracelet didn't work in Glimmer!"

"I don't think it does, Paddy. But there's a chance that we may not be in Glimmer anymore. That arch may have brought us back to the real world. That's why the bracelet worked this time. Paddy, we're in the real world again!"

Paddy's eyes widened with excitement. "We've done it, then, Molly! That's grand!" He frowned, seeing Fionn. "Who is this?"

"Oh, Paddy, this is Fionn. He was helping me look for you."

"And he's from the real world, then?" Doubt lingered in Paddy's eyes.

"That's the interesting thing. Fionn, would you mind showing Paddy …?"

Fionn nodded and pulled his blond hair back to reveal his ears. Paddy gave an involuntary gasp. "You're *Sidhe?*" he exclaimed in wonder.

"Did you say Shee?" Fionn repeated. "Do you mean the fairy folk?"

"Aye. Sometimes it's part o' the fairy's name, like the Ban*shee*. Have ye lived among the good people, then?"

The boy shook his head. "I've lived my whole life with my family. They're human enough, but they never acted humanely toward me. They were always beating or kicking me, and I never had enough to eat."

"Then it's a changeling ye are," Paddy muttered.

"A changeling?" Molly jumped into the conversation. "What's a changeling?"

"It's getting late," said Fionn. "Why don't you come back to Master Finegas' house with me for the night? Paddy can tell us about changelings on the way."

"That's a grand idea," Paddy smiled. "I'm tired o' walking these forests."

Molly helped Fionn gather his firewood from where he had dropped it. Paddy picked up a few remaining sticks, and they set out. The sun cast long shadows through the trees as they followed Fionn into the woods.

"Now, tell us about these changelings, my friend." Fionn gave Paddy an encouraging smile.

"Gladly!" Paddy began his tale. "The fairy folk have difficulty birthing their children. Many are born with deformities or other physical problems. Often the fairies will bring the babe to the real world, and exchange the sickly fairy for a healthy human child. Then they raise the human child as their own.

"The fairy child left behind is known as a changeling, because it was changed for the baby that the fairy wanted. The fairy casts spells to make the changeling look human."

"That would be cool to have a fairy in the house," Molly grinned.

Paddy did not smile. "Changelings are often seen as an omen o' bad luck, for they cry and disturb the household. They are never filled, and eat all o' the food there is. The enchantment wears off in a few weeks, and the family sees some changes. Their ears will return to their normal pointed shape, and usually their legs are as thin as a bird's legs. Changelings are generally shunned by humans."

"The last part you got right," Fionn nodded. "But I never ate up all the food."

"And you don't look deformed, and your legs aren't skinny like a bird's!" Molly felt herself blushing as she said it, and she quickly looked away.

"That's true," Fionn said, "if anything my family was jealous of me. They probably knew I didn't really belong to them once they saw my true ears. I guess the disguising spell wore off, like you said."

"The only thing I can't figure out," Paddy mused, "is why any fairy would exchange you for a human in the first place! It makes no sense, ye bein' strong and healthy. And not bad looking, eh, Molly?"

"Well, that's enough about changelings for now," Molly said briskly. "How did you come to be here, Fionn?"

Fionn kicked at the grass as they walked. "About two months ago, I decided I wouldn't take it any more. I got some extra food from the cupboard — I figured they owed it to me for back pay, so to speak — and ran away one night. I walked and ran for two days before I stopped."

"Did your family try to follow you?" Molly asked.

"I honestly have no idea. I was always a better tracker than any of my 'brothers'. If they are looking for me, they haven't found me yet."

"How did ye survive on your own?" Paddy inquired.

"I didn't have to for long. I tried to kill a deer, but I only had a knife." He patted the sheathed blade at his side. "Needless to say, the deer got away. Fortunately for me, Finegas the druid was watching me. He was amused, and after he heard my story he offered me food and a bed as his apprentice. He has been my master these past two months."

"Does he treat you well, then?" Molly asked hesitantly.

"Aye, that he does," Fionn smiled. "You'll see for yourself tonight at dinner. He'll be pleased to have guests."

They neared a neat stone cottage nestled in the woods. A lamp shone in the window, and the merry sound of bubbling water revealed a river nearby.

"So what's for dinner?" Paddy asked, licking his lips.

"The same as always," Fionn replied cheerfully. "Salmon."

chapter ten

The Salmon of Knowledge

Fionn, Molly and Paddy entered the small cottage. A wiry man, past his prime in years but looking very athletic, was stirring a pot over the fire. He turned to see the three enter. "Fionn! You didn't tell me you were bringing company!" His smile reached from ear to ear. "I had a fine catch today, there will be plenty of food for everyone!" He nodded at the three glistening salmon lying on the kitchen table.

"That's grand, Master Finegas!" Fionn smiled. "I just met my new friends this afternoon, over by the old arch."

"The old arch?" Finegas scowled as he stirred. "That's an evil place. Why were you over there?"

"Master Finegas, both of them came through the arch. They appeared as if by magic."

Finegas ceased his stirring and stood up. "Well, we have very special dinner guests then. Go and start the fire to cook the salmon, my boy, and I will make them welcome."

Fionn nodded. "We left the wood we gathered by the fire pit outside. I'll come back for the salmon once the fire is hot." He nodded reassuringly to Molly and departed.

"Come over by the fire, children, so I can keep this pot of cabbage from burning," the druid said, sniffing the contents of his pot as stirred. "Where are you from?"

Molly and Paddy found seats on two low stools by the fireplace. "Paddy's from County Clare, and I'm from Chicago," Molly said.

Finegas shook his grey head. "County Clare I know, but where is this Chicago?"

Molly looked concerned as she said, "It's in America. We're in Ireland, right?"

"Aye, in Donegal. I know nothing about an America. Fionn said you came through the arch?"

"Yes," she nodded. "We were in Glimmer, and were trying to return to the real world. To here, I mean. Paddy's magic worked when I got here, so we think this is the real world. The arch must have taken us between the two worlds." Molly suddenly looked embarrassed. "Gosh, you must think I'm crazy, talking about magic and stuff!"

Finegas closed his eyes. "Not at all, my dear. Magic I understand. Ah, someday all of the rest will be plain to me. If only my old hands were quick enough to fulfill the prophecy sooner."

"What prophecy?" Paddy asked.

The old man opened his brown eyes and fixed them on his guests. "Long ago, when I was a young man, a fortune-teller told me that I would catch the Salmon of Knowledge one day."

"The Salmon of Knowledge? What's that?" questioned Molly.

"At the headwaters of all the rivers of Éire grow nine hazelnut trees. These trees possess all of the knowledge in the world. As the hazelnuts drop from the trees, they fall into a well where they are eaten by a salmon. Thus all of the knowledge of the world passes into the salmon, which is then called the Salmon of Knowledge. Whoever eats that salmon will have all of the world's knowledge passed to him.

"For these many years, I have fished in the River Boyne which lies just beyond this cottage to catch the Salmon of

Knowledge. I have become very good at catching salmon, but I have not caught the one salmon that I truly desire." Finegas sighed. "Perhaps it is my destiny to gain this great knowledge only so near the end of my life that it will be of little benefit to anyone."

"You are a good man, from what Fionn has told us," Molly said earnestly. "Surely you will catch the Salmon of Knowledge. Fionn thinks the world of you!"

The old man smiled. "He's a good lad, isn't he? It's a pity that his family is so blind not to see his value and goodness. Fionn is becoming my arms and legs as I begin to grow feeble."

At that moment the door opened and Fionn came in. "The fire's going, I'll get the fish on," he grinned. "How are you doing in here?"

"I was just telling them about the prophecy," Finegas said.

"Oh, yes, you will catch that wily salmon one of these days, Master! I'm sure of it!" He lifted his armload of salmon and went out again, tugging the door shut with his toe as he left.

"Bless that boy!" Finegas said. Molly turned and saw a tear trickle from the old druid's eye. He wiped it away and turned to stir the cabbage again. "He cooks a wonderful fish on the spit, you'll see!"

————————

Dinner was delicious, as the druid had promised. The salmon was flaky and bursting with flavor from the spices Fionn had rubbed into it before cooking it. Even the cabbage was tasty to Molly, who was getting tired of energy bars.

They relaxed with hot tea afterward, and the conversation turned to plans for the next day. "You'll be wanting to get back to Clare and Chicago, I reckon," Finegas said as he sprinkled another lump of sugar into his tea.

"Do you have a phone, or know where I can use one?" Molly asked. "I really need to call my folks and let them know I'm all right. Although I don't know how I'm going to explain it."

Finegas and Fionn looked at each other blankly. "What is a phone?" Fionn asked.

Molly felt a tingle run up her back. "Either you guys live in the most isolated part of the entire world, or ..." she looked at Paddy. "Or maybe when we traveled back in time in Glimmer, when we came back over to the real world, we *stayed* back in time."

"Aye, that would be a problem," Paddy agreed.

"Why don't you rest up tomorrow and leave the day after?" Finegas suggested. "Fionn will be drying fish; you can take some of it with you when you leave. It's something you can carry easily and it won't spoil."

"Since we can't get to a phone anyway, that sounds like the logical thing to do." Molly sighed. *At least I'll have another day to stay close to Fionn,* she thought. *He is so cute.*

The next day dawned beautiful and clear. Fionn woke Molly and Paddy early to start drying the fish. "It takes all day, we need to get started!" he grinned. Soon they were sitting around the smokehouse taking in the salty aroma of the salmon.

"What do you do in Chicago, Molly?" Fionn asked.

"I go to school, mostly, except for the summer and Christmas break. Last summer I came to Ireland, which is where I met Paddy."

Fionn nodded. "My family would never send me to school. Perhaps Master Finegas can teach me after he catches the Salmon of Knowledge."

A sudden commotion from the direction of the cottage brought them to their feet. "Fionn! Fionn! Come quickly, my boy!"

They sprinted to the cottage to find Finegas walking toward them, dripping wet, a beautiful golden salmon raised above his head.

"I've got it! I've got it! At last, I've caught the Salmon!" he shouted. The old man seemed to dance toward them in his excitement.

"Master, are you sure this is the One?" Fionn asked happily.

"This is the true Salmon of Knowledge! Oh, my, I'm quite out of breath. Take the fish and cook it for me, so I may eat it. I must rest for a minute!" He handed the salmon to Fionn and crawled to a nearby tree stump to sit. "Go on, go on and cook it. But you must not eat of it yourself or taste it, is that clear, my lad?"

"Absolutely, Master!" Fionn's eyes shone. "I will prepare this fish to be the best you have ever had!" Turning to Molly and Paddy he said, "Come with me, we'll prepare the spit right away!"

Soon the salmon was turning on the wood spit over the crackling flames. The smell of broiled fish filled the meadow.

"Wow, that smells good," Molly said. "Finegas is in for a treat."

"I'm so happy for him! He's waited such a long time. He deserves this." Fionn frowned as he saw a blister pop up on the salmon's skin. "That won't cook properly," he said, and pressed his thumb to push the blister flat. "Ouch!" he exclaimed, and pulled his thumb back quickly, sticking it into his mouth.

"What happened?" Molly asked, fearful that Fionn had hurt himself badly.

"It's hot!" he groaned. "I just burned my thumb. It will be all right." He sucked on his thumb to ease the pain.

Soon the fish was broiled to perfection, and Fionn placed it on a great wooden platter with some fresh carrots. Molly and Paddy followed him in a grand procession to the cottage as he proudly held the great salmon aloft. Molly opened the door for him and he set the fish before Finegas, who was already sitting at the table with his knife in hand. "Master, your salmon!" Fionn crowed.

Finegas licked his lips and started to put his knife to the salmon when he stopped. He glanced around, then he looked at Fionn. Fionn stood expectantly waiting for the feast to begin. Finegas, however, was looking at Fionn's eyes.

"Fionn, my lad, your bearing is different. Have you eaten of the fish, now?"

A look of horror crossed Fionn's fair visage. "Oh, no, Master! I would not! I only cooked the fish for you!"

Finegas continued to stare at the boy. "I believe you, Fionn, for I know your heart. But your eyes are changed. Tell me all that happened when you cooked the fish."

Fionn appeared grief-stricken at being questioned further, but he answered. "I put herbs and spices on the fish to flavor it. There was a blister that came on the skin, and I pressed it flat so it would cook properly. That was all."

"And what did you press it flat with, my son?" The druid's eyes were keen on the boy.

"I used my thumb, sir. It was hot, and I burned it, and put it in my mouth without thinking, to cool it."

Finegas laid his knife on the table and pushed the platter away from him. "You've tasted the skin of the Salmon of Knowledge, Fionn my loyal boy. Only the first person who tastes the Salmon may benefit from eating it. Your composure, your eyes were changed when you entered the room. It is no good to me now. Take the Salmon, and eat it all."

"No! Master, the Salmon is for you! You caught it, just as the prophecy said you would! I will not take this great gift from you!" Tears filled Fionn's blue eyes.

Finegas sighed. "I did not tell you the full prophecy, my son. The prophecy indeed said that I would catch the Salmon of Knowledge, but also that I would not eat of it. Today the prophecy has come true. Fionn, *you* are the one truly intended to eat the Salmon of Knowledge."

Fionn replied, his voice quavering. "You are right, Master. I know what you say is the truth. I knew it the moment I put my thumb to my mouth."

Finegas smiled sadly. "Call me Master no more. Eat the Salmon, and leave me. The knowledge of the whole world is yours, Fionn. I can teach you nothing else. Your destiny now lies beyond this humble cottage."

Fionn walked to his old master and laid his hand gently on the old man's shoulder. "This will I tell you, Finegas my dear friend. One day you will catch another Salmon of Knowledge, and you will eat it."

The druid looked up at the young man through tear-filled eyes. "Bless you, Fionn. The world will be better for your spirit in it."

Somberly Fionn, Molly and Paddy left the cottage through the back door, Fionn again carrying the platter of fish. He set it on a rough table outside, and then started to eat it.

"Fionn! How can you do that?" Molly cried. "Poor Finegas is heart broken back there in the cottage, and you're eating the Salmon like nothing has happened!"

He looked up from his meal, chewing slowly. "Finegas is wise. He understands that the quest for knowledge is not always as easy as you want it to be. There are setbacks and there are surprises. But the quest must be made, for even in the trying you learn wisdom. I must eat this fish, or all of its wisdom will be lost forever. Now I will be able to use this wisdom for good."

Paddy put his hand on Molly's arm. "He makes sense, Molly. Who knows that he hasn't gained the knowledge that will help us get back home?"

"If we *can* go back home. Paddy, we may be trapped in a different time now, even if we are in the real world."

"That's what we thought at the Columbian Exposition, too, but it wasn't the case."

Molly sniffed. "I don't think we are in Glimmer now, because the magic is working again. It's just strange that no one knows anything about telephones."

She looked over at Fionn, who was finishing off the last bite of the salmon. He licked his fingers, smacking his lips at the flavor. "Well, maybe all of that knowledge can help us," she said hopefully.

Carefully she pulled out her heart-shaped locket and opened it. Her parents' pictures matched her memories of them. Her mother's eyes sparkled in the picture as they did each day now. Her father's picture still smiled out at her, but a new memory had crept in. Work-dad was crowding into her mind, a threat to all the good things that had happened since last summer. She had seen him, met him even, and he was real — wasn't he? Molly had to get home, no matter what. She snapped the locket closed with more force than was necessary.

A muffled banging sounded on the front door of the cottage. Loud and ugly voices shouted, "Open up, old man! We know he's in there, and we've come to claim him!"

"Who is it you're talking about?" came Finegas' voice. "I live alone here, have for years."

"We have a witness who says you've taken in that thief Fionn, who stole from us and ran away, about two months ago! Let us in!"

Fionn put a finger to his lips for silence. "It's the O'Doherty brothers," he whispered. "They've come for me at last." He led them away from the cottage toward the woods. They had almost reached the first trees when a figure in a white shirt carrying a club rounded the corner of the house.

"There he is!" he shouted. "He's goin' into the woods!"

"So much for that plan," Fionn growled as they ducked behind some bushes. "They are too close. We won't be able to shake them without a head start."

Molly thought hard, and then gulped. "Both of you come over to me. Get really close."

Paddy looked at her blankly, then he frowned. "Molly O'Malley, what are ye thinkin' …"

She pulled out her leather pouch and removed the golden coin. She felt the briefest sensation of floating. "The magic is back," she whispered.

Footsteps were thrashing through the underbrush now. The O'Dohertys would be on them in a moment.

"Closer!" Molly hissed urgently. Paddy and Fionn pressed as close to Molly as they could. Molly stretched her arms around both Paddy and Fionn's necks.

"Fionn, do ye know if this will work?" Paddy asked fiercely.

"I don't think the Salmon has had time to digest fully yet," Fionn admitted.

"Then you'll both have to trust me. Oh, I hope this works!" Molly dropped the coin into the pouch.

The lead O'Doherty boys crashed into the glade where the three fugitives had been kneeling. All they saw was a golden haze that lingered for only a moment.

chapter eleven

The Bog of Sorrows

Scattered clouds played hide-and-seek with the late morning sun. Crickets chirped from their secret places as a frog gave a deep, throaty croak from his perch on the edge of the bog. Light reflected from the surface of the moist peat where the sun reached the ground.

A golden kaleidoscope appeared at the forest edge nearby, quickly materializing into three silhouettes kneeling close together. The golden sparkles disappeared, leaving behind the forms of a tall, blond boy, a small girl with red hair, and a leprechaun.

Molly stood up and looked around. "Did we get away from them? I don't see or hear them."

Paddy sat down on the turf and slammed his hat down beside him. "I'll say one thing, Molly, when a fella travels with you, ye never know what to expect. Ye know that ye've taken us back into Glimmer."

Molly nodded. "I didn't have a choice. I'm pretty sure we were in the wrong time anyway, and I thought we might find a way to get back to our own time from the Glimmer side. We haven't invented time-travel in the real world yet." She pulled the coin from the pouch and held it for a moment. "Yep, the magic's gone again."

"You mean we're in the fairy world?" Fionn asked.

"I thought *you* were supposed to know *everything* now! I can't believe you ate that entire Salmon of Knowledge." Molly rolled her eyes at the memory.

"I was hungry for *knowledge*," Fionn smiled. "Anyway, it takes eight to twelve hours for the body to fully digest a large meal, so I may not absorb all of the Salmon's knowledge until then."

"We're trying to get to the Fairy Queen's castle, Castle Tiarnach. When I put the coin into the pouch, I tried to concentrate on a castle in Ireland that had an association with fairies," Molly sighed.

"Oh, that's grand!" Paddy exclaimed. "That could put us at just about *any* castle in Eire!"

"Well, somebody had to do something! Those O'Dohertys almost got Fionn!" Molly snapped.

They fell silent and looked across the bog. A grey heron flew up from a stand of slender reeds, flapping its wings while its long legs trailed behind it. The frog croaked once more.

"What is this place?" Molly asked.

"This is the Bog of Sorrows," Fionn replied.

Molly and Paddy turned to look at him. "I'm not even going to guess how ye knew that," Paddy said.

"I couldn't tell you," Fionn replied. He put his thumb in his mouth. "That's interesting. When I put my thumb in my mouth — the thumb that I burned when I first tasted the skin of the Salmon — it helps me remember things better."

"It makes you look silly!" Molly giggled.

Fionn raised an eyebrow. "Do you want me to look dignified, or do you want to know which way it is to the castle?"

Molly stopped in mid-giggle and Paddy leaped to his feet. "There's a castle nearby?" Paddy demanded.

Fionn nodded and held his moist thumb up to the wind. He nodded after a moment. "The direction that the wind is blowing from." He jabbed his thumb toward the north. "Through the bog, unfortunately."

———————

Hours later, the three travelers slogged their way slowly through the Bog of Sorrows. Fionn led them across narrow paths where they did not sink too deeply.

"Fionn, how do you know where to go in this mess?" Molly asked.

"I can't give the Salmon all of the credit for this," Fionn admitted. "I've always had a good head for tracking and finding my way around the woods and swamps. It comes from spending as much time as possible hiding from my family, I guess."

"Molly, do ye have anything to eat in your backpack?" Paddy asked. "We were so busy watching Fionn eat that salmon, we didn't get anything for lunch ourselves."

"You're right, Paddy, we didn't. I'm getting a little hungry myself. Fionn, can we stop a minute for a snack at least?"

"All right, but let me find a spot that's not going to sink under us when we stop. It's a little soft through here."

After a few minutes Fionn felt comfortable letting them stop. The peat gave way to solid turf where a great willow tree planted its roots in the spongy soil.

"One 100 Grand bar, Paddy, that's all!" Molly said as she handed him the candy bar wrapped in red paper. "We're running low on food, since we weren't able to get any of that dried salmon Fionn was making."

"Oh, all right," Paddy grumbled. His attitude improved instantly as he ate his candy. Fionn looked on with interest.

"Did you want something, Fionn?" Molly asked.

"Oh, no, Molly, I'm fine." He raised his fist to his mouth and belched. "I just ate that whole salmon. I'll be good for a while. I was just watching Paddy. Is that a magic candy bar? It seems to have a strange effect on him."

Molly sighed. "I think it's just a sugar rush. He's not very big, and it seems to make him kind of loopy if he eats too much."

Paddy leaned back against the willow's trunk. "Fionn, do ye know why they call this the Bog o' Sorrows?"

Fionn's face darkened. "Are you sure you want to hear it?"

Molly sat down next to Paddy and unwrapped a granola bar. "We may as well. You can talk while we eat."

"Very well." He sighed, glancing up briefly at the puffy clouds overhead. "Long ago, after the castle was built, a man named Jake Brennan and his new bride Orla came to this area to make their fortune in the world. There was no bog then; the land was green and fertile as far as the eye could see.

"Jake found a place that looked especially fine, except for a lone hawthorn tree that had grown up in the middle of a rich field. Now everyone knows that a hawthorn tree growing by itself is a fairy tree, and it is extremely unlucky to cut it down, for the fairies will have their revenge. But Jake Brennan was a fool who despised the tales of the good people. 'Fairies are nonsense,' he said, 'They'd best not mess with Jake Brennan!' and he cut the hawthorn tree down to build his house in the middle of the field.

"No sooner had he built his sturdy cottage, when the next day he stepped onto his porch to see all of his fine land turned into a watery bog. His house began to sink, and within a week it had disappeared completely into the bog. Jake was a stubborn man, and he built another cottage on the same place. It too sank into the muck. He built a third cottage on the spot, and it stayed up, though no one knew how.

"Now the people that lived in the area told Jake that he had ruined their livelihoods, for their farmland had turned to marshland, and their crops rotted away. 'I'll not let the fairies beat me,' Jake boasted. He took to cutting blocks of peat out of the bog, and that supplied all of his needs."

"What is peat?" Molly asked.

"Peat is made up mainly of plants that have partially decayed. It forms in wet places like the bog here, as it absorbs a great amount of water. It's rather spongy. When you take it out of the bog and squeeze the water out, the dried peat is very good for burning. In fact, once you start a peat fire, it's very hard to put it out. That's how Jake made his living, selling peat that was burned to cook barley for making whiskey, or just used to heat homes during the winter. It's also grand to use when planting trees or flowers, because it's so rich in nutrients." Fionn looked up again as a cloud covered the sun.

"Go on with the story," Paddy urged as he nibbled his candy.

"Jake thought that he had beaten the fairies, because he was using the peat created by the bog to survive. One day he came home after a hard day of cutting peat, and opened the door to find a pig in the kitchen. 'Why those meddlesome fairies, puttin' a pig in me house!' he roared. He picked up a stick and chased the pig around the house until it ran outside. It fled straight into a nearby pool and became stuck.

"The pig began to squeal in terror, and Jake saw that the poor creature was beginning to sink. 'Serves ye right, sink back to the blasted fairies that sent ye! You've left my kitchen a mess!' Jake turned to walk back to the house, when the pig's squeals gave way to a woman's cries. Looking around, he saw his beloved Orla trapped in the mire where the pig had been. 'Orla!' he cried, and he tried to rescue her. But it was too late. Jake himself sank deeply as he tried to wade out to her, and he could not reach her in time. Poor Orla sank into the bog, and Jake was left to himself with only the noises of the marshland and his sobs."

"Boy. This really *is* the Bog of Sorrows." Molly had stopped eating her granola bar.

"So I guess the fairies had enchanted Orla to look like a pig?" Paddy asked cheerfully, popping the last of his candy bar into his mouth.

Molly shot a stern look at the leprechaun. "Maybe only *half* a candy bar from now on. You're waaay too cheerful."

Fionn nodded. "Jake finally gave up and moved away. His cottage eventually sank into the bog like the first two did. The townspeople and farmers moved away to find work, and the castle was abandoned."

He looked up at the sky again. The wind blew his hair around his face. "And we'd better be moving quickly, if we expect to make it to that castle before this storm hits."

Dark clouds rolled over the marsh as the three travelers picked their way across the soft ground. Thunder rumbled in the distance as sharp spikes of lightening lit up the horizon. The wind rippled the surface of the thin layer of water, making it difficult to tell the difference between safe footing and watery peat. Every few steps Fionn paused to study the path ahead, sticking his thumb in his mouth occasionally.

"You're doing great, Fionn," Molly encouraged. "How much farther is the castle?"

The boy pointed ahead of them. About a quarter mile away, a dark structure rose from the surrounding swamp. The walls were squat and heavy, looking more thick than tall. In the center rose a grim-looking keep, with battlements ringing the top. No flag flew, but there were some carvings or statues on the highest part.

"It's getting darker; in addition to these clouds, the sun is about to set. We'll probably get a little wet, but I think we can get to the door before the worst of the storm hits." Fionn reached back and took Molly's hand. "Be careful through here; it may be worse close to the castle. Are you doing all right, Paddy?"

"Aye, I'm a bit lighter, so it's not too bad." Paddy grinned. "Although I could use another 100 Grand bar."

"NO!" Molly and Fionn said together.

The wind began to howl as they approached the gate. A simple drawbridge lay in front of the door, its wood somehow intact, reinforced with iron bands.

"Why would they leave the drawbridge down?" Molly shouted over the wind.

"You have to close the drawbridge from the inside!" Fionn shouted back. "When they left, there was no one remaining to close it!" He paused for a moment, staring at the door. Then he shook his head and stepped onto the drawbridge.

"Come on, it's safe!" Fionn pulled Molly onto the bridge and motioned for Paddy to hurry. Drops of rain began to fall, quickly becoming enormous in size. They stepped under the ancient portcullis, which may or may not have been rusted in place, and sought shelter under the entryway.

"Should we make for the keep?" Paddy asked. "At least it would have walls."

"No telling if it still has a roof," Fionn replied. "If we're going to check it out, we'd best do it now. This storm is only going to get worse."

They sprinted across the cobble-stoned courtyard to the main door of the keep, which hung open on its hinges. Pushing inside, they found the roof above them somewhat intact. A hallway led to their right and left, and a short set of stairs climbed to a massive closed door in front of them.

"Let's check out the hallways first. I'll take the one on the right." Paddy ran off before anyone could respond.

"Should we go after him?" Molly asked.

Fionn shook his head. "At most, it will go in a circle around the inside of the keep. We'll probably meet him faster walking to our left."

Molly and Fionn walked down the hallway, which grew darker, having no windows. Molly pulled out her flashlight and shone it into the darkness. "Oh, it's a dead end. All the stones are finished, so it looks like it was planned that way, not just a wall falling over." Molly sighed.

Fionn stared at her flashlight. "What is that you're holding, Molly?" he asked.

"It's my flashlight. You know what a flashlight is …" she stopped and turned to look at him. "You really don't know, do you?" She switched it off and began walking back toward the entrance. "We really *are* in a different time."

Paddy was waiting for them. "Is it a dead end down that way, too, then?" he called. Fionn nodded. "Well, I guess we should try this door in front of us. If one o' you would do the honors; big doors are a bit of a problem for me!" Paddy bowed and swept his hand toward the door.

Fionn stepped up to the door and tried to push it open. "It's locked," he said.

"Umm … Fionn?" Molly said. He looked around at her, and she pointed to a key ring hanging on the wall beside the door.

Fionn smiled good-naturedly and got the keys. "Ah, yes, these might make it a little easier." He fanned them out and pushed one into the keyhole. Turning it, he grinned at the click that followed. "Let's try this again." Putting his shoulder to the door, it swung inward easily.

Molly stepped inside, expecting to have to adjust to the darkness. Instead she gasped and grabbed Fionn's arm.

Across the room sat an old man. Books, musty with age lay in crooked stacks all about him. A table, carved with serpents and lizards glowed with candles burning brightly beneath vials of multi-colored liquids. And above all, the most marvelous aroma of food filled the air, making their mouths water.

"You're too late," the old man said. "It's already gone."

chapter twelve

Castle Dúr

*t*he old man calmly took a sip from his teacup. "You're too late," he repeated. "He's come and taken it — oh, you're back. I hadn't expected to see you."

Molly and Paddy followed the man's gaze to where it rested on a very confused Fionn. "M-Me? Back? What do you mean, sir? I've never been here in my life, I swear!"

The man stood and approached the protesting boy. Pulling his spectacles lower on his nose, he gently brushed Fionn's hair back from his ears and then peered closely at his face. "Humph," he finally muttered. "You're right, you're not him. Almost his double, though, from across the room." He paused and fogged his glasses with his breath, wiping them with a corner of his robe.

"No, it's certain you're not him. You have the look of a fairy in you. That's all the difference I need to know." He turned his attention to Molly and Paddy. "What are your names, now?"

Molly and Paddy exchanged glances. "I'm Molly, this is Paddy and this is Fionn. Fionn's ears should be enough to tell you that he's fairy-born," Molly said.

"Well, it's not just the ears, for the other one had them, sure enough. I've been around enough fairies to know." He pushed his spectacles back up on his nose. "It's the eyes. You can always tell by the eyes."

"Then it's true!" Molly cried. "Fionn, you *are* a changeling! You were left in the place of a human baby that was taken! You're from the fairy world!"

"There's more to this than that, Molly," Paddy offered. "Most changelings are left because they are born weak or crippled. That's why the fairies exchange them for bright, healthy human children. But look at Fionn! I've never seen a healthier looking young man! Why would any fairy leave him behind and take a human instead?"

"I think I may be able to answer that question," said the old man. "But first, let's get something to eat. It's a long story, and you must be famished after your journey."

He gathered some bowls and mugs from the ancient cupboard. He filled four mugs with golden mead from a clay jug. The bowls he carried over to the large black cauldron in the corner.

The cauldron appeared ordinary enough, a bit largish, old cast iron by the look of it. A liquid bubbled merrily in it, which was what was giving off the wonderful smell of good food. A thick wooden pole stuck out of the brew. Then Molly noticed the odd thing about the cauldron: There was no fire beneath it.

"How — how is that possible?" she stammered. "There's no fire under your pot, yet it's boiling like mad!"

Unfazed, the old man calmly ladled a thick stew from the cauldron, and then handed a steaming bowl to each of his guests. "You'll have to excuse the mess, I don't often get visitors. There's no room on the table just now. Oh, my, I forgot the spoons! Just a moment." He shuffled over to the cabinet and retrieved the wooden tableware.

"I think he's a bit nuts," Paddy whispered.

"Nuts? No, my little friend, I still have all of my marbles. That's why they keep the door locked." He smiled crookedly as Molly gasped. "No need for you to fear me, young lady, and I haven't forgotten your question. Eat the stew, you'll find nothing else like it!" He took a bite from his own bowl and smiled at the taste.

Molly took the spoon and hesitantly tried the stew. It was even better than the smell. Potatoes, carrots, onions and peas were mixed in a rich broth with generous chunks of savory meat. "Mmm… this is good! What kind of meat is this?" she asked.

"Lamb," Fionn said. "A traditional Irish stew, cooked to perfection. Now that we have solved that mystery, I'd like to talk about the other half-dozen mysteries our host has introduced in the past few minutes. Can we start with what is this place, and who you are?"

The man nodded and motioned for them to sit down. "My name is Alvaro Giovanni, and my part will be clear shortly. We are in Castle Dúr. The castle was abandoned when the bog formed, but a fairy named Vroknar claimed it for his own dark purposes."

"What dark purposes?" Paddy asked.

"Vroknar wanted to be the king over all the fairies. Unfortunately for him, he was not of the royal bloodline. Yet his thirst for power could not be quenched. So he formed a deadly plan to gain the throne."

Alvaro finished his stew and set the bowl aside. "Vroknar came to me in the guise of a businessman who needed my services. I was suspicious, as my interests were mainly in the field of alchemy."

"Alchemy?" Molly sat up straight. "Isn't that where you try to turn ordinary things into gold?"

The old man smiled as he looked at Molly. "Yes, that's true. We also discovered how many different chemicals could be used to change things during our experiments. It was this

96

latter ability that Vrokner was interested in, as he seemed to already have gold in abundance. Gold which I had not yet been able to create and which I needed to continue my search for the secret of alchemy.

"He brought me here to this castle, and in this very room we created …" Alvaro shivered, as though a chill wind had suddenly blown through him … "a terrible thing."

"What kind of thing?" Molly leaned forward.

"Vroknar had found a rare fairy-being, both ugly and noxious. It had the unique power to resist fairy magic, while having a terrible hunger of its own for that magic. My job was to create potions and creams that changed the creature, making it deadly to fairies, but harmless to humans. We called it *Anamith.*"

"Soul-eater," Molly whispered. Paddy's face turned white.

"Wouldn't that make it deadly to Vroknar, too?" asked Fionn.

"Yes, but it couldn't be helped. That's why he needed me to be his shield. As a human, the creature could not kill me." Alvaro's eyes unfocused for a moment. "Not … kill."

"But it kills fairies?" Fionn demanded.

"With merciless efficiency. It has a long tongue that lashes out and grabs its victim. Fairy folk are helpless in its grasp, and it draws them into its mouth and devours them. The power of its attack is indescribable."

"Mr. Giovanni, you said that it couldn't kill humans. You looked a little worried when you said that. What does the Anamith do to humans?" Molly clenched her hands into fists as she asked the question.

"Molly, the Anamith seeks souls, and the life that is in them. Although he cannot eat your soul, he can feed on your thoughts — your dreams, your most precious memories." Alvaro shivered again. "It's not pleasant."

"So how did you restrain this monster?" Fionn asked.

"I constructed a cylinder with a sliding panel, like a dark lantern." Alvaro smiled grimly. "This was the darkest lantern in history, perhaps."

Fionn nodded with understanding. "A dark lantern can be opened as little or as much as you like to let out only the amount of light that you want, or no light at all when you close it. Your lantern is designed to hold the Anamith prisoner, allowing only enough of an opening to attack when the holder chooses."

"Yes," Alvaro chuckled. "I put an extra lock on the sliding panel for good measure. I called it the Lantern of Souls, because it eats the souls of its victims."

"It's a terrible thing you've created, Alvaro Giovanni," Fionn said soberly.

"Yes, it is." Alvaro was quiet for a moment. "At first I believed Vrokner when he told me that he needed the Anamith to destroy the fairies and the pagan beliefs that supported them. I felt as if I was on a holy mission. But as the Lantern of Souls was completed, I realized that Vrokner was only interested in killing certain fairies — the fairies that stood between him and the throne. He only needed me to wield the Anamith, as it was too dangerous for a fairy to hold." The old man winced with disgust. "He needed a human to do his dirty work."

"So did you do his dirty work?" Fionn asked without smiling.

"One day the Fairy Queen's guard showed up at the castle. Rumors had traveled to the royal court, and the Queen was determined to deal with the crisis. Vroknar ordered me to turn the Lantern of Souls on the guards. At the last moment, I turned and faced Vroknar, and opened the lantern door." Alvaro breathed heavily. "He never had a chance. The Anamith caught him and dragged him into its mouth. Then I closed the door tightly."

"This story is really getting scary," Molly said softly.

"The royal fairy court passed judgment and decided that the Lantern of Souls needed to be locked away. They decided that Castle Dúr was the ideal spot, for both the Lantern and its creator." Alvaro adjusted his glasses and smiled glumly. "At the same time, they used the opportunity to solve another problem."

"What problem?" Molly asked.

"Molly, you noticed earlier that the cauldron with the Irish stew had no fire under it. That is Dagda's cauldron. It can summon any type of food you desire, and will never run out until you change it to a different type of food."

"Dagda's cauldron! Here!?" Fionn's eyes were wide.

"What is Dagda's cauldron?" Molly asked. "It's just a magic pot, right?"

Fionn shook his head. "This I know from eating the Salmon. Dagda's cauldron is one of the four treasures of Eire!"

"I don't understand! What are the four treasures of Ireland?"

"Let me explain, Molly," Paddy offered. "Ye remember when I told ye about the *Lia Fáil* at Tara?"

"Oh, yeah," Molly said. "I do remember. You said that the Stone of Destiny was one of the four treasures of Eire. So Dagda's cauldron is another one of the treasures?"

"Aye," Paddy said. "When the Tuatha Dé Danaan, the fairy folk first came to Eire, they brought the treasures with them, one from each o' the four cities they came from."

"So Dagda's cauldron can make whatever food it wants and cooks it itself?" Molly asked. "That's why there's no fire under it?"

"Fionn, why don't you go take that pole out of the stew?" Alvaro suggested, his brown eyes twinkling.

The boy walked to the cauldron and lifted the long pole from the stew. As it came out, the stew stopped boiling.

"Will ye look at that!" Paddy exclaimed.

The end of the pole held a large spear point, which hissed and steamed as the remaining stew ran off of it. Soon it was clean and dry.

"It can't be," Fionn said in disbelief.

"You'll see in a few minutes," Alvaro smiled.

Now the spear point began to glow a dull red color. Molly could feel the heat radiating across the room. "What's going on?" she cried. "Why is the spear getting hot?"

"If I'm not mistaken," Fionn said, "I hold another of the great treasures of Ireland in my hands. We will know shortly." The spear point was now white-hot and giving off a significant amount of heat.

"Any time, Fionn my boy," Alvaro chuckled. "This is the only castle we've got." Even as he spoke a bolt of lightning leaped from the spear point and burned a large hole in a wall tapestry. Another bolt snaked across the room and blew a stack of books onto the floor, leaving the pages smoldering.

Fionn plunged the spear head back into the stew. After an initial hiss of steam, the contents resumed their steady boiling.

"There's little doubt," Paddy said with a sigh of relief. "It must be the Spear o' Lugh."

"Who is Lugh?" Molly asked.

"He was a great hero of the Tuatha Dé Danaan. His spear glowed white-hot in battle and shot lightning bolts from it. No enemy could stand before it."

"Nor any friend behind it," Fionn added with a grin.

"Only the cauldron of Dagda seems capable of containing it," Alvaro said. "The fairies decided to store both of them here to protect them from theft or misuse."

"How would storing them here protect — oh." Molly broke off in mid-sentence. "The Lantern of Souls would make it too dangerous for any fairy to try to steal the treasures."

"Exactly, young lady!" Alvaro beamed.

"Excuse me," Fionn said, "but I have a question about that. Where is the Lantern of Souls now?"

Alvaro's face darkened. "As I said when you came in, you're too late. It's gone."

"Gone where?" Fionn demanded.

"Gone with your near-double. Where, I don't know. It was just yesterday that he came to me, unlocked the door and started asking questions. He pretended to be a fairy, but I saw right through that, of course. He had the pointed ears, but you can tell by the eyes. He was as human as I."

"My near-double." Fionn put his thumb to his mouth.

"He had some story about needing a present for his mother. Then he grabbed the Lantern — I had left the key to the panel lock right beside it, and he took that, too — and ran out the door, locking me in again. I pounded on the door, shouting that he didn't know what he was doing! I only heard him say something about how his mother the queen would be pleased." The old man sighed and peered at Fionn. "But you know, don't you Fionn?"

Fionn pulled his thumb out of his mouth, wiping it carefully on his sleeve. "It is clear that the boy is intended to look like me." Paddy and Molly stared at Fionn in amazement. He smiled grimly. "It gets better. I am not the changeling. He is."

chapter thirteen

Cillian

The boy struggled out of the woods and into the clearing. He stopped and set his burden on the ground, a large metal cylinder with a domed top that reflected the afternoon sun. He stretched for a moment, rubbing his arm ruefully. Looking up, he admired the stone walls of the castle rising above the treetops. "Ah, Tiarnach, it's good to see you again." He lowered his gaze to the humble bungalow in the clearing. "Can't say I'm happy to see *you,* though." He ran his fingers through his thick brown hair and shook the sweat from his eyes. "Well, I'd best get on with this."

He hoisted the metal container by its handle and trudged toward the cottage. Stepping onto the low stone porch, he rapped hesitantly on the heavy wooden door. "Lady Corrigan?" he whispered.

The door flew open to reveal an old fairy woman bent with age, remnants of tangled grey hair clinging to her head. She scowled at the lad and hissed, "Cillian! Where have you been? I expected you yesterday!" She grasped the boy by his ear and tugged him into the room.

"You've got it then?" she demanded as she closed the door tightly behind them. Her eyes grew wide as she saw the metal container. "Ahh, the Lantern of Souls! It's here at last …" She reached out to touch it, as if to see if it were real, but stopped short and drew her fingers back with a suppressed shudder. She turned to the boy.

"What took you so long? Taking your jolly time along the road, were you? Three days for a trip that should have taken two!" She smacked the boy smartly on the back of his head. He drew back with a whimper.

"No, milady, truly I hurried as much as I could! The Lantern is heavier than I thought, and it took me almost two days to come back. I've bruises on my legs and back from carrying it, bumping with every step …"

"Spare me your pitiful excuses!" The fairy-hag leaned close and smiled, showing a grin that was missing some teeth. "If it's rest you want, perhaps I can turn you into a nice fat slug and set you on a pretty rock in the garden! Wouldn't it be wonderful to laze about until someone sprinkles some salt on you?"

Cillian's eyes grew wide with fear. "Oh, no, milady, I've no right to complain! But I did get back before the celebration, and I did get the Lantern for my mother!" He looked down and muttered softly, "I did do something right."

Corrigan cackled hoarsely. "*You* did something right? Remember who you are, brat! You're nothing but a lowly human posing as a fairy — and a fairy prince, at that! If it weren't for my charms and constant effort to make you appear as a fairy, the Queen would have you punished beyond your worst nightmares!" She leaned close to the trembling boy, her foul breath hanging in the air. "You owe me, Cillian, you owe me everything!"

"Y-Yes, Lady Corrigan," the boy stammered. "I didn't mean to offend …"

"Oh, stop whimpering and clean up! Do you want to look like a Prince at your mother's birthday party or not?" Cillian scampered to the kitchen sink and poured a bowl of water. "You need to get out of those traveling clothes, boy. Your court clothes are in the other room. You're fortunate that I plan these things so your feeble mind doesn't have to worry."

Corrigan walked around the Lantern of Souls, keeping a respectful distance. "You have the key, boy?"

Cillian dried his face on a towel. "Yes, ma'am. It's here in my pocket. Did you want to open it now …"

The old fairy whirled around. "I told you, it's a surprise for your mother! You will *not* open this present until you give it to her at the party! Is that clear, you stupid boy?"

"I won't open it! I'm sorry!" He started for the other room. "What's in that lantern that is so special, anyway?"

Corrigan grinned and her eyes shone. "Trust me, Cillian, when she sees what is inside, she will just die!" She chuckled softly. "Change now, you have a couple of hours before the party starts. You must be ready!"

———

One hour later Cillian strode toward Castle Tiarnach dressed in his court finery. He carried the Lantern of Souls with him, trying not to bump it against his clothes. As he approached the gate, he heard a low whistle from behind a bush. He hesitated before calling out, "Who's there?"

"It's just old Tagnus, doin' some final trimming," a voice returned. An elderly fairy wearing a worn oversized felt hat stepped out from behind the bush and nodded approvingly at Cillian. "You're looking fine for your mother's birthday, ye are. And you're not coming empty handed, either!"

Cillian breathed a sigh of relief. "Tagnus. Don't you ever stop working on the gardens and bushes? You keep everything looking so wonderful! I wish I had half your talent." He smiled at the groundskeeper and raised his hand holding the lantern. "Just a little something I picked up."

"I'm sure she will love it. Been over at Lady Corrigan's place again, lad?" Tagnus tucked his shears under his arm and mopped his brow.

"Aye." Cillian looked away quickly. "She — was giving me tips on how to behave at the party."

"She always has taken a special interest in ye, giving ye the best possible training. She was practically your nursemaid for many years." Tagnus looked toward the setting sun. "You're a bit old for a nursemaid now, Prince Cillian. You've grown into a strong young man, if ye don't mind me sayin' so."

"Thank you, Tagnus. I appreciate that. Maybe …" Cillian's eyes focused on the castle wall. "Maybe I can do something that will make my mother think more highly of me." He looked down at the lantern in his hand. "Maybe tonight."

Tagnus scowled as he pulled his hat down low. "Cillian," he said softly as he came near, "I hear things, ye know, while I'm tending the grounds. I've heard —" he looked around to see if they were being watched — "I've heard Corrigan say things to you that no one should say to any person, let alone a prince. It's a crime to give the title 'Lady' to that woman, I say! Why do ye let her treat ye that way, lad? Why don't ye tell your mother what is going on?"

Cillian looked startled, then panicked. "Oh, I can't, Tagnus! I can't, you don't understand!" He dropped the lantern and grasped the old man's shoulders with both hands. "Please, Tagnus, swear that you won't breathe a word of this to the Queen! You'll only make things worse, you don't understand!"

"All right, lad, all right!" Tagnus gently took Cillian's hands and squeezed them. "If ye don't want me to say anything to the Queen, I won't for now. But you think about it, yah?"

The boy nodded. "I've got to go. Thank you, Tagnus!" He picked up the lantern and made his way to the gate, the tin casing bouncing against his leggings despite his best efforts.

Making his way through the entrance he nodded greetings to the leprechauns standing guard and walked across the courtyard to the inner keep. The great double doors were opened wide as the court nobility arrived for Queen Meb's birthday party.

Cillian stopped to straighten his collar. "Well, here's to making a good impression," he whispered. He touched the key in his vest pocket to make sure it was still there. No point in having a present that can't be opened. Then he stepped into the throne room, holding the Lantern of Souls by his side. It seemed for a moment that the Lantern moved on its own as he entered. But of course that was impossible.

chapter fourteen

Pursuit

ionn led the way through the thick woods. They had left the Bog of Sorrows behind hours before, and Molly was not sorry to find solid ground under her feet once again. Paddy jumped and skipped to keep up with their rapid trek north.

"Fionn, I hate to ask this, but can we take a short break? I really need to catch my breath!" Molly puffed. Fionn glanced back and nodded, taking a final look at the ground and trees before sitting down on a mossy boulder.

Paddy fidgeted nervously. "I feel bad about locking Alvaro up in that castle again," he admitted. "Wouldn't he have been helpful in getting the Lantern back?"

Fionn shook his head. "Alvaro is too old now to keep up with us. The boy had almost a day's head start on us. And remember, it was Alvaro's idea to lock him in again. That's what he agreed to when the fairies imprisoned him the first time. He has found his honor after all of these years, I think. You often learn more from your mistakes than you do from your successes."

"How about you, Paddy?" Molly questioned, eyeing the leprechaun who was dancing up and down. "Are you doing all right?"

Paddy grinned in reply. "Just keep passing me those 100 Grand bars, and I'll have enough energy to keep up! I'm just worried that I'm not contributing anything besides eating up your stock o' candy."

"Well, why don't you try this?" Molly suggested. "We know that your magic doesn't work here in Glimmer because you're used to pulling the power over to the real world instead of using it directly. Can you practice your magic using the power directly? It might come in handy."

"Aye," Paddy nodded. "I'll do that."

Molly stretched and yawned. "Thank you, Fionn, for leading us. I wouldn't have a clue which way to go."

Fionn smiled. "My woodcraft is coming in handy, isn't it? Plus, I think the Salmon of Knowledge is fully digested now. I know the way to Castle Tiarnach, which is where I think the boy and the Lantern are headed."

Molly leaned forward with interest. "If you have all knowledge, where are they now? Is he really going to the Castle?"

Fionn shook his head. "I only know what knowledge the hazelnut trees had before they dropped their nuts into the well. Where the boy is now is something that has happened since the nut fell from the tree. But it seems likely that he is headed to the Castle. All of this knowledge —" he rubbed his temples — "everything is crowded together. It will take a while to sort it all out, I think."

Molly nodded and smiled. "I hope so. Headaches are no fun. We better get going again, though, or — Paddy?!"

Paddy had succeeded in making his 100 Grand candy bar grow to the size of Molly's bed back in Chicago. "I did it! I did it! Oh, this is grand, isn't it Molly?" he yelled, dancing around the huge wrapper like a child.

"Paddy, you can't eat that! That's — pretty incredible, though, you got the hang of that growing spell quickly."

The leprechaun stopped cavorting and turned to wink at the red-haired girl. "The spell's only temporary. It'll shrink back down in a minute." Even as he spoke, the bar returned to its normal size. He picked it up and put it back into his pocket.

"Molly's right," Fionn said, getting to his feet. "We need to keep moving. We have to get to the Castle before the boy gives that thing to the Queen." He paused for a moment. "The Queen — is *my* mother." Tears filled his eyes as he looked at Molly and Paddy. "*My* mother …"

"And we need to save her. It'll be all right, Fionn. Let's go." Molly gave his hand a gentle squeeze, and he squeezed back.

Fionn wiped the moisture from his eyes and took a deep breath. "Yes, let's go." He led the way into the woods where only his eyes could follow the footprints, broken branches and bent leaves that marked his near twin's passage.

It was late afternoon, but the sun still floated in the cloudless sky when they saw Castle Tiarnach above the trees. They entered a clearing with a small stone cottage.

"He was here, but he left in this direction," Fionn indicated. "There was another as well, a smaller fairy, probably a female. She left, too."

"Did he take the Lantern with him?" Molly asked breathlessly.

"I believe so. The footprints are the same depth as when we followed him from Castle Dúr. He has changed shoes — to a pair of dress boots. He's going to the party."

"Are we too late, then?" Paddy asked worriedly.

"The tracks are fresh, very fresh," Fionn said as he stood up. "Let's follow them."

The three sprinted through the remaining woods toward the outer wall surrounding the castle grounds. They had almost reached the gate when a figure stepped out in front of them. "Here now, where do ye think you're goin' in such a rush?"

"We're going to the party," Molly gasped, "isn't everyone?"

"Not everyone is invited to the party! And I don't even know who ye are …" His voice trailed off as his gaze fixed on Fionn.

Fionn stared back at the old fairy man in the floppy hat. "That's twice now I've seen that look," the boy ventured. "You know him, don't you? The boy who looks almost like me. But he has …"

"Darker hair," the man finished for him.

"He's in danger!" Molly whispered. "And the Queen is in danger, too! We have to stop him!"

The man spun to face Molly. "Why? What has the lad done?"

"He has a weapon, a terrible thing that looks like a lantern all made out of tin." Fionn's eyes were dark. "It holds something that the fairies thought they had locked away forever, but it has been released now. Or it soon will be. The boy thinks it's a present for the Queen …"

The old man's eyes opened wide with horror. "Cillian! Oh my boy, what has that devil done to ye?"

"What devil?" Paddy pressed.

"Corrigan, that foul nursemaid to the Prince! It's she who has told him to give it to the Queen." He turned to Fionn, his eyes brimming with tears. "She's a cruel, heartless beast who treats the lad like dirt. But she holds some power over him, I don't know what."

"Probably the secret that he is human." Fionn nodded at the man's gasp. "What is your name, my friend?"

"I am called Tagnus. How do you know this is true?" Tagnus was visibly shaken, but doubt still lingered in his eyes.

Fionn placed a steady hand on Tagnus' shoulder. "Because the boy you call Cillian was a changeling placed in my cradle. I am Fionn, the true Prince and heir! I was taken to a human family that I only recently escaped from. We do not have much time, Tagnus! Will you help us?"

"A changeling?" Tagnus shuddered. "A *human* changeling? But why — o' course, I can't deny my eyes, Cillian and you are almost twins. Cillian ..." He turned and beckoned to them. "Come this way. There is a service entrance around the back. You'll never make it past the guards at the main entrance."

They followed the gardener to a secluded door cleverly masked by a row of bushes. "Here," Tagnus pointed. "Go through this door. Cross the garden to the main castle; there is a small door there. Take the stairs to the left and go up one level. You'll enter the East side o' the throne room."

"Thank you, Tagnus," Molly said as Fionn opened the service door. "We'll do everything we can to save Cillian."

"Thank you, my dear." He choked back a sob. "Hurry, now!"

Ducking through the low doorway, the three ran across the grassy space to the castle wall. Suddenly Molly felt a violent jerk around her ankles and she nearly fell. Fionn and Paddy had stopped, too, and were standing still in the middle of the garden.

"What happened?" Molly asked Fionn. "I can't move my feet!" She looked down at the ground. "The grass is all grown over my feet, and I can't move them — omigosh! It moved! The grass *moved!*"

A shadow fell across the trapped rescuers. They turned to see a small fairy woman, dressed in fine clothes, her matted grey hair spun onto her head like the start of a cotton candy stick. She grinned at them, revealing an unnerving smile with some teeth missing. "Well, what do we have here? Three statues in the garden! I don't recall seeing them here before. I wonder, did Tagnus put them here? I'm going to have to have a talk with that lazy gardener, he's starting to leave things where they shouldn't be!"

Fionn remained unperturbed, as though being trapped in the middle of a garden were something that happened every day. "And you would be?" he asked gravely.

"Why, my dear boy! Don't you remember me?" She cackled softly. "I'm Lady Corrigan. Corrigan, the next Queen of the Fairies!"

chapter fifteen

Soul Eater

Molly leaned as close to Fionn as she could to whisper. "Do you know how to get loose from this grass?" Fionn gave a tiny nod.

He folded his arms and addressed Corrigan. "Why would you think that I would remember you? I've never seen you before in my life. And judging by your manners, I'm not sure I would have wanted to."

Corrigan's eyes flashed. "I see that your time among the humans has not taught you a proper respect for fairies," she growled. "You were born *here,* boy, in this castle, in that very room!" She stabbed a gnarled finger at an upper tower window, then rubbed her hands together in delight. "I switched that human brat Cillian for you, put *him* in your place. And I left you in the human world. Treated you well, did they?"

Fionn grimaced. "If your intent was to harm me, you chose well. The O'Dohertys are a pack of cheats and bullies who never wasted a chance to cause me pain."

"Harm you?" she laughed. "You idiot boy, it was never about you! It was all about getting a human under my influence, someone in the palace itself, someone who would not be suspected. And I succeeded! Thirteen long years, but now Cillian is accepted as the Prince! And *you* are nothing but a statue in the Queen's garden." Corrigan spat on the ground.

Molly turned and whispered to Paddy, "We're going to need a diversion in a minute. Can you think of something?"

The leprechaun's eyes flicked to the old fairy woman and back to Molly. "Aye," he whispered back, his lips barely moving.

"Yes," Fionn nodded, "Your quickgrass is very effective. It grows instantly where you throw the seed. Wonderful for filling in the bare spots."

"Oh, so you know about quickgrass," Corrigan grinned broadly, showcasing her ruined teeth. "How much do you know about Cillian?"

"Cillian? Oh, he's harmless. Someone else is pulling the strings, someone who is behind all of this scheming." Fionn stifled a yawn.

"Bah!" The old woman dismissed him with a wave. "You have your beautiful face and a noble physique. I was not blessed with a goodly appearance even in my youth. I was always plain, some would use harsher words. What I *was* blessed with, however, was perseverance."

"You stole me from my mother! You put a changeling in my bed! That is not perseverance, that is evil!" Fionn raised his voice as he responded.

"You were not the first," Corrigan chuckled. "I must have laid a thousand changelings in cradles, mewling fairy children that were good for nothing, and brought back lovely humans to their new fairy families. You were different. I stole Cillian for *me!* I replaced the Queen's son with my own creation! And mark me, Cillian is mine! He fears and obeys me! For years my magic spells and enchantments have maintained his fairy appearance, hiding his true nature from all except me. You were only a leftover nuisance, a puzzle piece from the wrong box. What a delight it was to drop you off with that cruel family on the other side of the arch. I watched them for months. Oh, they were so wretched I couldn't believe my good fortune! To deliver the Queen's son to such lowlifes!"

"So you used the arch that connects *Fannléas* with the real world. That's how I got there, and that's how Molly and Paddy got there." Fionn's face flushed with anger now. "But why did you do it? What do you have against my mother, the Queen?"

Corrigan laughed. "Meb always had the power over me. Poor Corrigan always had to tend to the children, to wait on her royal highness." The fairy woman's eyes glistened. "But let me tell you what makes me superior. I am willing to wait for what is mine. Then I have the resolve to take it! I cannot win others over to my will by gentle flattery. But all beings respect power. I will *have* that respect. The Queen will soon be no more, and Corrigan the nursemaid will be ruler of all the fairies!"

"What respect? You think you have earned respect when you force a child to do your bidding?" Fionn practically sneered. "Only a coward would send a child instead of going herself."

"You're a fool!" Corrigan's eyes darted toward the castle. "Cowardice has nothing to do with it. The Ana — " she broke off in mid-sentence. "Some things require a human."

Fionn nodded. "A human to do your dirty work. What will happen if the Anamith can't be controlled? What if it escapes? Have you even told Cillian what it is he carries?"

Corrigan's eyes widened. "Who are you? How do you know of the Soul Eater?"

Molly whispered, "Now, Paddy!"

A flash of silver rolled across the manicured lawn, growing taller and taller as it spun. Within seconds it was taller than a wagon wheel, a giant Columbian half dollar with the engraving of the Santa Maria spinning around as if caught in a whirlpool as it bounced toward the evil fairy.

"What devilry?" Corrigan screeched as she leapt out of the way. The half dollar rolled past and fell over, crushing a bed of petunias.

"I'll get you for that — " she began, turning toward the leprechaun. She didn't get a chance to finish. A 100 Grand bar as big as Molly's bed flew through the air and caught her full on. The force carried her to the ground where she kicked and fought under its weight.

"Fionn, what do we do now?" Molly urged.

"Quick, give me your jacket!" Fionn drew his knife and stretched out on the ground to reach her feet. "Hold the jacket over the quickgrass, so it's in the shade! Quickgrass can't grow without sunlight." He sliced through the entangling grass around her shoe, and then reached for her other foot. Behind them they could hear the sounds of paper ripping over Corrigan's muffled curses.

"I'm free!" Molly cried. "Let me help you, now!"

"Molly." She froze at the seriousness in Fionn's voice. "You have to go. It has to be *you*."

She stood for a moment until she realized what Fionn was saying. "You're right," she whispered. "It has to be me." She spun and raced for the castle door.

"Stairs to the left and up one level, stairs to the left and up one level …" Molly repeated as she ran up the worn stone spiral stairs. She heard the door slam below her and the sound of feet pounding up the stairs. *Hurry!*

Molly reached the top and found heavy curtains drawn across the entryway. She searched for the edge of the cloth and finding it, quickly pushed herself through the opening. The smoky aroma of fire made her catch her breath, as the light of a dozen torches painted a bright flickering warmth on the walls. The room was larger than she expected, at least twenty feet wide and about forty feet long. She found herself halfway along the length of the long wall. To her right a beautiful fairy sat in an ornate chair delicately carved with leaves and flowers.

Her clothes were stitched with glittering thread, and a circle of jewels wrapped her head. *The Queen!*

Molly looked for Cillian and found him directly in front of her, in the very center of the great hall. He looked almost exactly like Fionn, except that his hair was darker. Cillian was bowing low, the center of attention. Even now, with every eye upon him, he looked uneasy. The metal cylinder he held gleamed dully in the torchlight. He pulled a small lock away and started to slide the door open on the Lantern of Souls. "And now, Mother, I present this wonderful gift to you."

"Cillian!" Molly screamed. Cillian's eyes darted toward her. "Cillian, don't!"

Molly heard a rustle behind her and whirled to see the curtains part again. "You filthy brat!" Corrigan hissed as she entered. An ugly smear of chocolate streaked her face, and her fingers dripped caramel. She stepped forward, stretching out for Molly. Then she froze, looking past the girl, her eyes wide.

Molly looked back at Cillian. The double interruption had made him turn toward them. "Lady Corrigan?" he whispered. He didn't notice that the door to the Lantern continued to slide open, unbidden.

From the depths of the Lantern Molly could see two red dots glowing — *glowing!* — that were clearly not from a flame. The hair on her neck stood up and she felt cold, so very cold. A low rumble escaped from the Lantern, and Cillian looked down at it in surprise.

Corrigan screamed.

Something shot past Molly's head at a terrific speed, something long and black and slimy. It stretched from the open door of the Lantern of Souls and fastened itself around Corrigan's neck.

Corrigan's scream was cut off and her eyes bulged in fear. She looked for a second at Molly, a look of utter loss.

Then the old fairy nursemaid was flung around the room like a rag doll. She seemed weightless as the thing from the Lantern threw her against the walls and the floor, whipping her in tight circles that made Molly dizzy just to watch.

As suddenly as it began, it was over. The long black thing retracted into the Lantern, and Corrigan's body was impossibly crumpled and pulled inside with it. Her feet vanished into the black interior, and the red dots reappeared.

"That — that was its *tongue?*" Molly gasped.

Cillian dropped the tin lantern and it crashed to the floor, rolling to a stop on its side. He took a step back, his face ashen with an expression of horror. The fairies in the room had also retreated and the Queen sat immobile on her throne, clutching the carved wooden armrests. The attack had taken only a few seconds.

A tiny hand with stubby fingers reached out of the Lantern to grasp the edge of the opening. A thick foot stretched out to touch the floor, and a short, round, somewhat shapeless body oozed halfway into the throne room. It was a deep charcoal grey color, covered with bumps and wart-like nodules much like a toad's skin. The squat rounded head was featureless except for the two glowing red eyes, and a gaping maw of a mouth that would have stretched from ear to ear if it had had ears. A hint of the terrifying black tongue flicked around its mouth as the Anamith looked around.

And turned to face the Queen.

"No!" Molly screamed, and ran toward the throne.

The Queen was frozen in place, as were all the attendants. Molly looked briefly into the Queen's eyes to see shock registered there. *Well, that figures. Everyone is in shock right now,* Molly thought. *I've got to get between that thing and the Queen* …

Molly turned and put her hands up just as the giant tongue lashed out again. Its fleshy mass struck her and seemed to separate into a dozen thick tendrils that wrapped around her head, face and hands. It did not jolt her severely as it had Corrigan, however. Tug and twist as it might, the flailing tongue could do little more than push Molly slightly from side to side. Alvaro was right, it was engineered to kill fairies, not humans.

But there was something else the alchemist had said …

Molly felt a hand on her shoulder, and turned to see who it was.

"Dad?!" she cried in disbelief.

"Yes," he said, smiling. "I've come to take you home."

"Home? What do you mean? How did you find me?"

He ran his fingers through his red hair. "You're not the easiest person to track down, that's for sure," he chuckled. "The important thing is that I'm here now to take you home from all of this. Come on." He stretched out his long fingers to take her hand.

Molly looked around her in wonder. Rocks were piled up into walls that formed a loose circle about her, and the remains of her lunch were spread on a nearby flagstone. "I'm in the ringfort? How can I be in the ringfort?"

"What did you do, fall asleep after lunch?" he laughed. "I hope you didn't get sunburned. It's a sunny day in the Burren for a change."

Molly still had not taken her father's hand. "I'm really confused right now. Where is Mom?"

Her father's face darkened. "Mom's still in the hospital, sweetie. I just came to bring you back home to Aunt Shannon's. She's been worried sick about you."

"In the hospital?" Molly cried. "But she got better, she was fine, and you took a different job so you could be closer to home! Everything was better!"

"Honey, she's going to get better, but it's going to take some time." He withdrew his hand and scratched his nose absently. "I need to get you home to your Aunt's and get back to work. These medical bills are eating us alive."

"No, no, it can't be ..." Molly shook her head, feeling the tears start to well up. "I couldn't have imagined it. Everything was working out so well!"

"And everything will work out, dear. You can stay at your Aunt's, take your walks up into the Burren, and have fun talking with your leprechaun. You like Ireland, don't you?"

Molly felt her breath catch in her throat. "What leprechaun?"

"Your friend, the leprechaun you met. You didn't think you could keep it a secret, did you?" He grinned at her. "You can't keep any secrets from me, you know." His eyes burned with a red glow for an instant, darker than his hair.

Molly felt her skin grow cold. "You." She whispered. "You're not my father."

"Of course I am, Molly," he smiled. "I work hard to support my family. You should love me for the sacrifices I make for you and your mother."

Molly shook her head. "It's you. You're the *Anamith*. You're in my head, you're reading my thoughts, and you're trying to steal my dreams. Alvaro said you were horrible." She shivered. "You're worse than I ever imagined."

"Come, come, Molly, you've created a world of your own where leprechauns and fairies and dragons exist and it makes you happy! I don't begrudge you that! Stay in your make-believe Ireland if you want to! Just don't try to box me in while I'm trying to be the best father I can be!"

"You're not my father!" Molly screamed as she leaped to her feet. "You're a horrible, disgusting creature that Alvaro made to kill fairies!" She stepped forward and pushed him in the chest. "You stay away from me! Get away from me!" She shoved him again and again, her fingers sinking into his chest as though it were made of silly putty. "I won't let you! I won't! ***I won't let you steal my dreams!***"

Suddenly she was not pushing her father any more, but a squirming, black mass of flesh that wriggled all around her head. "Oh! Get off of me!" Molly screamed, pushing the horrid black tongue back and back until she shoved it into the Soul Eater's great mouth itself. She looked into the monster's red eyes, sternly shoved the charcoal colored lump of terror back into the Lantern of Souls and slammed the door panel closed.

A hand appeared beside her, slid a small lock on the door and clicked it shut, pulling it firmly to make sure it was closed. Molly looked up into Cillian's sweaty face.

"Thank you," he said softly.

chapter sixteen

Forever

olly heard the quick shuffle of feet, and looked around to see what it was. A ring of spears circled both Molly and Cillian, their sharp points menacing. *Now what?*

"Guards." The Queen's voice floated evenly across the hall. "I appreciate your concern for my safety. It may have been more effective if you had used your weapons when the creature was attacking instead of waiting until after this girl imprisoned it in its cage, however."

It took the guards a few seconds to realize what the Queen was saying. Sheepishly they lowered their spears and backed away. Cillian reached his hand out and helped Molly to her feet. "Thank you," she smiled.

"You're welcome," he smiled back.

"Now, Cillian," the Queen stood and spoke more forcefully. "What is this thing you have brought into my throne room?"

Cillian's smile vanished as if the Queen had slapped him. "I — I don't know, ma'am, and that's the truth. I thought it was a present for you, that's what …" He stopped and stared down at the floor.

"That's what he was told, your Majesty," Molly interjected. The Queen turned to look at Molly with interest. "That's what Corrigan told him."

"Corrigan? What do you know of Corrigan? Tell me your name child, and why you are here!"

Molly took a deep breath. "I'm Molly O'Malley, and I'm not from Glimmer, I'm from the real world. It's a long story, but we wound up somehow at this castle in the middle of a big swamp, and this thing — " she looked at the lantern in disgust — "had just been stolen by Cillian. Alvaro, the man living in the castle heard Cillian say that it was a present for his mother, the Queen. After we followed Cillian here, Corrigan trapped us in the garden and told us all about her plan!"

"What plan?" The Queen's eyes were blue steel.

"The plan to murder you, your majesty, so Corrigan could become the new Queen. She sent Cillian in with the Soul Eater so it would kill you, but it ended up destroying her instead, and she needed Cillian because he's — " she paused and looked at the boy. "Cillian," she sighed, "you really need to tell her now."

Cillian shook his head violently, his eyes wide with fear. "No, I can't …"

"Yes, you can! Corrigan is dead! She can't hurt you anymore!"

"No, please …"

"Tell me what?" the Queen asked impatiently.

Molly gulped. "That Cillian is human."

Her words echoed in the chamber for several long seconds before the Queen spoke. "Human? You must be mistaken, my dear. Cillian is my son. He has been with me since birth."

"No, your majesty. Corrigan stole your son when he was a baby, and put Cillian in his place. She's been threatening Cillian for years with telling everyone that he's human so she could force him to do whatever she said. She needed a human because she knew the Soul Eater could not kill a human, it could only kill fairies. Corrigan told us herself." Molly looked earnestly at the Queen. "Cillian is not your son."

"Then where is my son?" the Queen asked, her voice trembling.

"I am here!" Fionn stepped through the curtain into the throne room. A few blades of quickgrass still clung to his shoulders. Molly caught a glimpse of a leprechaun peeking into the room from behind him.

The Queen looked from Fionn to Cillian and back again. She lowered herself slowly onto her throne. "Is this possible?" she whispered. "They could be twins!"

Fionn strode into the room and knelt in front of the Queen. "Yes, Mother, it is true. We look similar only because of Corrigan's enchantments that she cast on Cillian. I am your son." He brushed his long blond hair back to reveal his ears. "Cillian's ears will lose their enchantment within the week."

"My son. Not Cillian." The Queen spoke as if in a dream. "What is your name, child?"

"My name is Fionn," he replied. "I discovered my true heritage only recently, with the help of Molly and Paddy."

"Paddy?" the Queen asked. Paddy stepped timidly into the room and waved uncertainly. The Queen did not wave back.

"Everything under control here, Molly?" Fionn asked with a glance at the locked Lantern.

"Yes, but please don't let that thing touch me again. That was awful!"

"Your majesty," Fionn said, turning to the Queen, "this creature is the Anamith, the Soul Eater, which was created by the evil fairy Vroknar with the assistance of a human alchemist, Alvaro Giovanni. Giovanni perceived Vroknar's true intent to murder the then-fairy ruler, and turned the monster loose to devour Vrokner instead."

The Queen tightened her grip on the carved arms of her throne and stared at the Lantern as Fionn continued.

"It was deemed too dangerous to keep the Soul Eater close to any fairy, even contained in the Lantern of Souls, so both Giovanni and his creation were locked away in Castle Dúr, which lies within the Bog of Sorrows. The Soul Eater must be returned there without delay."

"You speak with great wisdom for one so young," the Queen murmured. "Who here knows the path to this dark castle?"

Fionn's eyes darted to Molly for an instant. "There are several who know the way, but only Molly and Cillian should take the Lantern of Souls back."

Molly felt her mouth drop open. "You have *got* to be kidding!" she said.

Fionn shook his head sadly. "I'm sorry, Molly. It's too dangerous for any fairy to transport the Soul Eater. Cillian knows the way back, and I think he is ready to perform a great service for his Queen."

Cillian was caught off guard. He looked confused, but saw that the Queen was looking at him. He squared his shoulders and knelt, his eyes downcast. "I would do anything for my Queen!" He dared to raise his eyes and added, "I have always wanted only to please you."

"Then it's settled!" the Queen cried, and clapped her hands once. "Provisions for Molly and Cillian on their journey! How many days will it take, Cillian?"

"It only took one day to get there, but two days to get back," Cillian said with a groan. "That thing is heavy."

"We can go faster if I help carry it," Molly offered. "But we have to have a pole or something to carry it with. I don't want to get any closer to it than I have to."

"While the preparations are being made, I would like to have an audience with my son, Fionn. Alone." The Queen took a deep breath, and Fionn bowed low before his mother.

It was late morning on the second day when Molly and Cillian came in view of Castle Dúr. The Lantern of Souls swayed slightly beneath the pole they carried between them.

"Oh, Cillian, can we set this down for a second? My shoulder is killing me where the pole sits."

"Sure, Molly." Together they gently lowered their burden to the ground. "I don't see why we can't just find a soft spot in this bog and set it there," he grumbled. "No one would ever find it."

"I wouldn't bet on it," Molly groaned, rubbing her shoulder. "It didn't touch you like it did me. That monster — " she shivered — "can live forever on the thoughts it steals. Plus, it needs to be inside the castle to keep the fairies away from the treasures unless they really need them!"

"That's right, you were telling me about those." Cillian found a fairly dry spot on the grass and sat down. "I was in such a hurry last time, I left before that old man had given me anything to eat from the cauldron. In fact, he was dishing me up a bowl from it when I took the Lantern. It made a good distraction."

"Well, we should be there by lunch time today. Irish stew sounds delicious right now!"

"Irish stew?" Cillian frowned. "When I was there, he was dipping out seafood chowder."

"Hmm … Oh, yes, Alvaro did say that it could make any kind of food you wanted. I guess lunch will be a surprise after all." She shook her arms to loosen her muscles. "Ready?"

They entered the castle and stopped before the keep's great wooden door. "The keys are still here," Cillian observed. "Let's see if anything is missing."

The lock clicked easily as Cillian turned the key, and the great door swung inward. The aroma of fresh cooked vegetables struck them immediately. "Alvaro? Mr. Giovanni?" Molly called. "Are you still here?"

"Where else would I go?" a tired voice answered from the shadows. "Who is it this time? Do you bring good news or ill?"

"It's me, Molly O'Malley, and Cillian, the boy who took the Lantern of Souls. We — we've brought it back."

"Back?" Alvaro whispered. "You succeeded in your quest then, my dear? It didn't kill anyone else?"

"It did kill someone, Mr. Giovanni," Cillian said. Alvaro drew a sharp breath. "It killed Corrigan, a wicked fairy who deceived me my entire life. She deserved to die!"

"Do not glory in vengeance, my boy," Alvaro warned sternly. "Those who use the Anamith to destroy others will reap only sorrow for themselves."

"It was an accident, really," Molly said. "But I have to agree with Cillian, if someone had to die, I'm glad it was Corrigan."

"Set the Lantern across the room there. That's right, as far away from me as you can. This calls for a celebration!" Alvaro walked to the cauldron and sniffed. "Vegetable soup? Let's have something special! Spaghetti with meatballs!"

The black pot changed from the merry bubbling of soup to the glop-glop-glop sound of spaghetti noodles in a rich tomato sauce. "You call that a meatball? Give me some meatballs, you wretched thing!" Alvaro kicked the large cauldron, and several giant meatballs popped to the surface.

"That's better," he grunted with satisfaction. "Forks today, Molly. Cillian, is it? Fetch some bread from the cupboard there, will you, lad? I baked yesterday."

Molly pushed the beakers of bubbling liquids carefully to the side to make room at the table. Soon they were eating the most delicious spaghetti and meatballs Molly had ever tasted. Cillian relished his food as well, even though it was unfamiliar to him.

"They're not really poisonous, you know," remarked Alvaro, twirling his spaghetti on his fork.

"What?" Molly asked, forgetting to chew for a moment. Cillian looked at his plate and slowly set his fork down.

"The tomatoes. Many people think that the tomato is poisonous to eat. I've run dozens of tests, and I'm reasonably certain that they are perfectly safe. Just the thing for a good spaghetti sauce, don't you think?" The alchemist slid his rolled up ball of noodles into his mouth, unconcerned.

Molly swallowed and relaxed her shoulders. "Oh, tomatoes! Of course they're not poisonous. I know that people used to think that tomatoes were poisonous hundreds of years ago, but ..." She paused again, looking worried.

"What is it, Molly?" Cillian asked.

"It's just a feeling I've had for a while. Finegas and Fionn had never heard of a phone, I haven't seen anything modern in like forever, and now most people think tomatoes are poisonous?" She shook her head. "Either Glimmer is not very modern, or I've traveled back in time, or maybe both. I'm worried about how I'm going to get back home."

Cillian looked glum. "We should ask my mother for help. She knows a lot about magic ..." he looked at Molly and grimaced. "Rats! I've got to get used to not calling her that now. The Queen is *not* my mother, and everyone knows it! I don't know what's going to happen to me! Will I be sent back to my human family?"

"I don't know, Cillian. We'll have to go back and find out. You helped recapture the Soul Eater by putting the lock back on the Lantern."

"Yeah, but I'm the one that let it out in the first place. I feel terrible."

Alvaro cleared his throat. "Well, Cillian could stay here with me. The only two humans who have ever released the Soul Eater! Keep an old man company!"

"I — I'll have to think about that, Mr. Giovanni. Perhaps my m — I mean, the Queen will send me here, but she didn't tell me to stay and not to come back. Thank you for the offer, though."

"We'd better get going, Alvaro," Molly said, dabbing her lips with a napkin. "Thank you for the wonderful meal!"

"Oh, you can't leave now! It will be nightfall soon! At least stay the night in the castle!"

Molly shook her head and looked over at the tin cylinder sitting across the room. "I don't want to spend any more time near that awful thing than I have to."

Alvaro's eyes seemed to stare through the walls of the castle. "I understand, Molly. Believe me, I truly understand."

Molly looked at the old alchemist as his statement sank in. "Oh, Alvaro, I'm sorry," she whispered. "I didn't think about you being here with the Soul Eater for ..."

"Forever." He finished her sentence. Not the way she was going to finish it. But after that, there was nothing left to say.

chapter seventeen

A Glow at Twilight

I'm not sure this was such a great idea," Molly said as Cillian helped her through another muddy spot. "The sun is almost down and it's getting really hard to see where to walk." She clicked her flashlight on to create a dim orange glow. "And my flashlight batteries are almost dead."

"We knew we'd be spending the night outside when we left," Cillian nodded. "But I thought we'd be out of the bog by now."

"Well, thank you for locking the door to the keep. I couldn't bring myself to do it, leaving poor Alvaro alone again with that monster."

"He did insist that we lock him in again. He really feels responsible for the Soul Eater." Cillian sighed and looked across the watery landscape. "Hey, is that a light?"

Molly strained to see where he pointed. "It sure looks like it! Let's go see what it is. Maybe somebody lives out here!"

"It's worth a shot," Cillian agreed. "I'm not looking forward to spending the night in the open if we don't have to."

The pair walked toward the glow which flickered in the twilight. "I think it's moving away from us," Cillian remarked.

"Look!" Molly said pointing. "Do you see a man?"

"Yes, he's holding a lamp or something." Cillian grinned at Molly. "At least *his* lantern is giving off light. Not like the Lantern of Souls that just sucks everything in."

"Don't remind me! Let's talk to him. Maybe he has a place where we can spend the night." Molly waved her flashlight toward the man. "Hello! Can you help us?" she called out.

"I don't think he heard you. He's still moving away. Do you want to follow him?"

"Yes, let's," Molly sighed. She switched her flashlight off. "I just hope the ground is firmer in this direction."

The half moon played hide-and-seek among the scattered clouds. Molly and Cillian were able to move quickly when the moon shone on the bog reflecting off the water, but they had to slow down when it ducked behind the clouds again.

"Are we getting any closer?" Cillian grumbled.

"I think so," Molly said. "Let me try calling to him again. *Hello! Can you help us?*"

The figure stopped and turned slowly toward them. He regarded them for a moment, and then he waved his light in a wide arc.

"Oh good, he *did* hear me! Come on!" Molly stepped forward and immediately sank knee deep into the bog.

"Molly, take my hand!" Cillian cried. He pulled her out and they looked at each other.

"That was close," Molly breathed heavily.

"Look, he's waving again. Let's go before he changes his mind." Cillian helped Molly to her feet and they continued toward the light, skirting the mire this time.

The man's features were shrouded in darkness. As they neared him, flickers of light from his small lantern lit the edges of his face.

"Good evening," Molly said when they were close enough to talk. "We got caught out here when it got dark. Would you have someplace where we could spend the night?"

"O' course, friends! I'll be happy to share what bit o' comfort I have with ye." He held his lantern near his face, which appeared gaunt and spectral.

"That's an interesting lantern you have there, sir," Cillian commented. "I don't think I've ever seen anything like it."

"It's a turnip, lad, just big enough to hold an ember to light me way. What do ye call yourselves, children?"

"I'm Molly and this is Cillian. Thank you for helping us, Mr. …"

He winked at her. "Just call me Jack," he chuckled. "Stay close now, the light isn't very bright."

They walked through the bog together; Jack's light casting ghostly shadows behind the trees as they passed. "How long have you lived out here, Jack?" Molly inquired.

"Oh, not long, not long," he replied. "I've moved around quite a bit since I met Mr. Tanas. Quite the gentleman he was, with a fine coat and hat, a fresh marigold pinned to his lapel. And what a businessman, too!" Jack laughed aloud at the memory.

"Did Mr. Tanas sell you something?" Molly asked.

"Sell? In a sense I suppose. He promised me a long and healthy life. Then he gave me a wrinkled old scroll to sign. No sooner had I penned me name than he roared with laughter and showed me the terms on the scroll." Jack whispered the words. "I had sold him my soul!"

"Tanas … T-A-N-A-S …" Molly's eyes opened wide. "That's an anagram!"

"An ana-what?" Cillian asked, bewildered.

"An anagram," Molly explained. "It's a word you make by mixing up the letters from another word. You can rearrange the letters from the word Tanas to read S-A-T-A-N … Satan! Is that it, Jack? Did you sell your soul to the devil?"

"Aye, that I did. I had to think fast. 'Well,' I said, 'you've tricked me fair and square. But I can't bear to live in hell for eternity without my family. Me son's up in that tree right now. I'd be obliged if you would go up and get his soul too, so we can be together.' "

Jack smiled slyly at Molly and Cillian. "There's nothin' the devil craves more than another soul, so o' course he shimmied right up that tree. I took sticks and laid them down to form several crosses at the foot o' the tree. Mr. Tanas let out a screech when he found there was no one in the tree, and a bigger screech when he saw the crosses beneath him. 'Jack, you miserable creature! Take those crosses away or you'll be sorry!' I folded me arms and said, 'I'll take the crosses away once you promise that you won't take me to hell.' He screamed and threatened, but eventually saw that I was serious, so he agreed."

"So that's how you got your soul back!" Molly said happily. "That must have made you feel good!"

Jack smiled. "I did feel good for many long, pleasant years afterward. Until I died."

Cillian stared at Jack with his mouth agape. "You … died?"

"Yes. I went to heaven, but they wouldn't let me in. You see, I did mostly bad things while I was alive, so I didn't qualify." He grinned wickedly. "So they sent me down to hell."

"Wait a minute," Molly interrupted. "This isn't making any sense. You just said that the devil promised not to take you to hell!"

"So I did, so I did," Jack chuckled softly. "And the devil — schemer that he is — *kept* his promise. He wouldn't let me into hell, either. I asked him, 'Where will I go?' He said I must walk the earth, as I was unwelcome in heaven and banned from hell; doomed to wander in darkness forever. He gave me only one small kindness; an ember from the fires o' hell to light my way. I had me turnip with me, so I hollowed it out and put the ember inside. Now it's just old Jack and his lantern."

"I don't like where this is going," Molly whispered.

"Oh, you're not going anywhere. You're going to keep me company on my long walk." Jack's laugh echoed in the dancing light from his lantern.

Suddenly the light vanished leaving Molly and Cillian in pitch blackness. They heard Jack's laugh drifting back from in front of them. "The light! Where did the light go?" Cillian cried frantically as he groped forward.

"No!" Molly screamed, reaching out for his tunic and yanking him back. "Cillian, don't follow him!"

"Why not?" he asked, breathing hard.

"Check the ground in front of you with your foot. Carefully."

Cillian slid his foot forward and it suddenly slipped into empty space. "Ahh!" he cried, drawing his foot back quickly. "A cliff!"

"It was just a guess," Molly murmured. "Do you remember when Jack first motioned for us to come to him, just before I fell into that bog pit?"

"You fell into a *lot* of bog pits. But let's say you're right. We're standing in the dark on the edge of a cliff and a crazy dead guy is trying to kill us. What do we do now?"

"I don't know, Cillian. If I were back in the real world, I could rub my silver bracelet and Paddy could find me."

"Well, why don't you try it now and see?" a familiar voice chuckled from the darkness.

Molly felt her skin prickle. "Is this some kind of trick? Don't move, Cillian!"

"I'm not moving. Who is it, Molly?" Cillian looked around helplessly in the dark.

"It's Paddy Finegan, or someone who sounds just like him," Molly growled. "All right, I'm rubbing the bracelet."

"Nope. Still nothing. Just as I expected. Turn your torch on, and then set it down so the beam will shine straight up, Molly," the voice said merrily.

Molly switched her flashlight on and stuck the back end of it into the soft dirt.

Suddenly the flashlight towered 15 feet above them, its fading orange glow now multiplied many times to illuminate the area. A weasel with a white underbelly blinked in the light. "Step away from the edge now," it said.

Gratefully Molly and Cillian retreated from the precipice and approached the weasel. "Paddy?" Molly demanded.

The weasel vanished, replaced by a leprechaun decked out in green and beaming from ear to ear. "I think I'm starting to get the hang of using magic inside Glimmer. Your torch should last long enough to guide Fionn here. See? Here he comes now!"

A hundred yards away they saw the flame from a torch moving toward them. Soon they were indeed joined by Fionn.

"What are you doing here?" Molly demanded.

"You want us to leave?" Fionn responded, his blue eyes twinkling.

"Not unless you take us with you," Molly said firmly. "How in the world did you find us?"

Fionn lit another torch and handed it to Cillian. "Paddy and I thought you could use some company on the way back," Fionn began. "We didn't want to get too close to you while you still had the Anamith. I had a feeling you wouldn't want to be too close to it either after you dropped it off at the castle. How is Alvaro, by the way?"

"Terrible," Molly sighed. "But he's determined to stay locked up with that thing. Paddy, may I have my flashlight back, please?"

"Aye, that's a bit large for your backpack, isn't it now?" Paddy hummed as he shrank the flashlight back to its normal size.

Fionn continued. "Anyway, we were watching for you when you veered off in a different direction. Paddy saw a light across the bog, so he transformed into a weasel and went to check it out. Weasels see better at night than we do."

The torchlight was bright enough to let them walk safely through the bog with both Fionn and Cillian scouting ahead for danger. Molly told Fionn and Paddy about their encounter with the mysterious Jack.

"Ahh, yes. Jack," Fionn murmured. "All Irish children know about Jack and his lantern. He leads unwary travelers astray to death and destruction with his glowing light. Sometimes he's just called the will o' the wisp. He's usually seen over bogs at twilight."

"I didn't know about him," Cillian said glumly.

"You were raised in the palace," Fionn responded. "Corrigan didn't have to threaten you with old Jack to make you do things. She had secrets much worse that she used to manipulate you. Don't be too hard on yourself."

"Why does Jack sound familiar to me?" Molly wondered out loud. "I've heard it somewhere before."

"People started making lanterns of their own by carving gourds and putting candles in them, to keep away evil spirits. They called them jack-o-lanterns."

Molly snapped her fingers. "That's it! Back home we have those at Halloween. Only we carve them out of pumpkins instead of turnips."

More lights appeared in front of the little party. Fionn led the way into a little clearing, where two tents were set up. A small campfire crackled cheerfully on the dry ground within a ring of stones.

"Here's home for the night," Fionn announced. "Paddy and I followed you down to the edge of the bog and camped out to wait for you. You two go ahead and change out of your traveling clothes, we have some clean clothes for you in the tents. You look like you've fallen into every mudhole in the Bog of Sorrows!"

"I think I did," Molly said ruefully. "Oh, Paddy, look at the mess I've made of your beautiful boots! They're caked with mud!"

"Mud will wash off, Molly dear, those boots are made to withstand more than a walk in the swamp. Give them to me, and I'll clean them off while ye change."

"Thank you Paddy, you're such a dear." Molly unlaced the boots and handed them to the leprechaun. "It'll be good to get into some clean clothes. I've been feeling yucky for days!"

"That's the least of our problems, Molly. We still have to figure out how to get back to the real world." Paddy shook his head as he began to chip away at the mud on Molly's boots.

"You may have more resources than you know," Fionn said mysteriously, "after all, you did save the Queen." They all turned to look at him. He shrugged his shoulders. "I can't give away all of the Queen's secrets, but since Molly saved her life, I think the Queen will be willing to help her."

"That's okay for Molly," Cillian whined. "I'm the one who is really going to be in trouble. I brought that Soul Eater right into the throne room! The — the Queen will probably throw me in prison or execute me now that I've helped lock the Lantern of Souls back in that castle. She won't have any need for a useless human. You're the Prince now, Fionn."

"Yes," Fionn said softly. "And the Prince knows your heart, Cillian. You have acted bravely under difficult circumstances. I am not the only one who has seen this."

Cillian looked up, hope lighting his eyes for the first time in days. "I think I'll go change. I want to look presentable when we get back."

chapter eighteen

Royal Gifts

althoughthe four travelers were weary, their spirits lifted when they saw Castle Tiarnach. The late afternoon sun hung in a glorious blue sky as puffy white clouds drifted by on a gentle breeze.

The main gate of the castle was thrown open, flanked by guards resplendent in their green livery. As the quartet passed by, the guards lifted their spears to form an arch for them to walk under.

A beautiful young fairy in a long gown greeted them in the outer courtyard. "Greetings to you, Molly, Cillian, Paddy and Prince Fionn. Is your task accomplished?"

"We took the Soul Eater back to Castle Dúr. It's locked away again, along with Alvaro Giovanni." Molly brushed back a tear as she finished her report.

The fairy nodded at Molly's report without changing her serious expression. "You are all invited to a royal feast in your honor. The feast will begin at sunset. Attendants will now take you to prepare."

"I'm invited too?" Cillian asked in amazement.

The fairy granted him a warm smile. "Yes, Cillian, you are definitely invited."

They were each whisked to separate rooms. Molly found that a great bathtub of dark wooden staves had been filled with hot, clear water. She quickly undressed and plunged into the water, relishing the heat as she scrubbed away the dirt. It had been way too many days without a shower. The soap held a fragrance captured from the forest, a wonderful scent that reminded her of spring.

After her bath Molly found a glittering gold evening gown waiting for her, and soft slippers that sparkled like the stars. She dressed and sat down in front of the mirror. She was struggling to pull her hairbrush through her thick red tresses when a young fairy maiden entered the room.

"Is there anything I can help you with, milady?" the fairy asked.

Molly set her hairbrush down and stared at the mirror. "Do you know anything about fixing hair?"

"It's what I spend my days doing, Miss," the fairy smiled.

Twenty minutes later Molly could not believe what she saw in the mirror. Her hair was combed straight and smooth, then drawn up to the back of her head where it disappeared in the delicate weave of a French braid. Yellow daffodils on either side of the braid completed the effect.

"Thank you!" Molly gushed. "It's beautiful! What is your name?"

"Jewel," the fairy replied.

"Oh, you *are* a jewel! I wish I could take you home with me!" Molly frowned at the thought. *I just wish I could go home!*

Jewel led Molly to a large hall where a long table was set with plates, goblets, candles and huge platters of food. Fionn, Paddy and Cillian were already waiting there. Cillian wore a light blue suit embroidered with silver thread. Fionn looked elegant in a suit of deep purple trimmed with gold. Paddy's green suit looked like new, and he had taken off his hat.

"Molly, ye look grand!" Paddy grinned broadly.

"You clean up pretty good yourself!" Molly replied, trying not to stare at Fionn.

A sudden fanfare of trumpets sounded and Queen Meb entered the hall. Her gown looked like hundreds of leaves sewn together, and the different shades of green rippled in waves as she moved. A thin circle of jewels sparkled on her brow.

The Queen approached the large chair in the middle of the great table. "Molly," she said, "you will sit at my right hand and Paddy beside you. Cillian, you will sit at my left hand and Fionn beside you."

Cillian nodded dumbly, in shock that he would sit next to the Queen. They went to their chairs where leprechauns wearing what Molly thought looked like miniature tuxedos seated them.

The Queen raised her glass. "A toast!" Everyone raised their glasses. "To Molly and Cillian, who imprisoned the Anamith once more! May it never be released again!"

"To Molly and Cillian!" cried all of the fairies around the table.

Cillian rose, and all eyes turned to him. "Your majesty, I would like to make a toast as well," he said. The Queen nodded. "A toast to Fionn and Paddy, who rescued Molly and me from an untimely end at the hands of Jack of the Lantern!"

"The will o' the wisp?" voices whispered around the table.

Cillian raised his glass high. "To Fionn and Paddy!"

"To Fionn and Paddy!" the fairies echoed.

"Well spoken, Cillian," the Queen said approvingly. The boy blushed crimson, bowed stiffly and sat down.

"Now, to the feast!" the Queen proclaimed.

Molly had never tasted such delicious fruits and breads in her life. There was chicken and something that Paddy said was rabbit, but she wasn't sure if she believed him or not.

Finally the food was taken away and the dishes cleared. Servants brought damp towels for the guests to clean their faces and hands. Everyone's eyes now turned to the Queen.

"I have a few things to say," she began. "Molly O'Malley, you have shown great courage in withstanding the

Anamith. I present you with this bolt of cloth woven on the fairy-looms of Tiarnach. It can be changed by simply saying 'water' and pulling it into whatever shape you desire. Then it will retain that shape when you say 'ice'."

One of the leprechaun butlers laid the folded cloth before her. The cloth was an unattractive olive-brown color. Molly picked it up and held it close to her dress. "Water," she whispered hesitantly.

The crowd gasped in amazement. "Look!" someone pointed. "It changed to a gold color, just like her gown, with sparkles and everything!"

"Oh," Molly said, "It's beautiful! Thank you so much!"

"The thanks are ours, Molly," the Queen smiled. "Now we will turn our attention to Cillian."

Cillian reddened and shrank into his seat.

"It has come to our attention that Cillian is not my true son. He is in fact a human that Corrigan placed in my son's cradle as a changeling. The question before us is what is to be done with this boy? Should he be sent back to his human family?"

Cillian shook his head *no*, his eyes wide with fear. Molly jumped to her feet and cried, "Please, your majesty! I've seen his family and they are mean and cruel! Cillian doesn't deserve to be put into their hands. It wasn't his fault that he was stolen!"

The Queen merely smiled at the interruption. "This has already been pointed out by Prince Fionn," she said, "and I agree with both of you. If we do not return him to the human world, where should he go?"

"Begging your majesty's pardon, he can stay here." The gruff voice came from the doorway.

"Tagnus?" the Queen said smoothly. "What does my faithful gardener have to say about this?"

The old fairy hobbled across the room, his cane tap-tap-tapping on the stones. "He should stay here with the fairy folk! It's all he has ever known!"

"But he has no family," the Queen protested gently.

"If it please the Queen, I'll take the boy." Tagnus' expression was set and Cillian wore an expression of pure joy. "I can use some good help tending the flowers and bushes. Cillian has often shown an interest in me work. So if he'll have an old fairy …"

"Yes! Yes! Of course I'll stay with you!" Cillian shouted. Then in a more subdued tone he added, "If your majesty thinks it wise."

"I find it very wise," the Queen smiled. "I am happy you want to stay with us after all that you have suffered."

"I'll make you proud of me, your majesty! I'll grow the most beautiful flowers in all of Eire!" Cillian looked as if he would burst.

"I am proud of you now, Cillian, and I'll look forward to seeing those flowers." The Queen nodded. "And now to the problem of Paddy Finegan."

Paddy was caught in mid-grin and immediately assumed a somber face with his hands clasped before him. "Yes, your majesty."

"I understand that you have confessed to stealing a coin from the Royal Treasury?"

"Yes, your majesty." Paddy's lips were a thin line.

"Arthur, would you please tell me again what you found in your inventory of the Treasury?"

A portly leprechaun with a quill pen tucked behind his ear waddled up and unrolled a musty scroll. "All o' the gold is accounted for, your majesty. Not a single coin is missing."

"Do you still have this coin, Mr. Finegan?" the Queen asked.

"No, I gave it to Molly."

"Ah. I see. Molly, do you have this coin now?"

Molly looked at Paddy, then back to the Queen. "Not with me. It's on the table in the room where I changed. It's next to my hair brush."

The Queen nodded and a fairy ran off. He returned in a few minutes clutching a golden coin.

"Is this the coin, Molly?" the Queen asked.

Molly looked at the coin. The mountains on one side, the woodlands on the other were burned into her memory. "This is it," she sighed.

"Arthur, is this coin from the Treasury?" the Queen demanded.

Arthur squinted at the coin carefully. Finally he raised his head. "Aye," he said, "it's from the Treasury. But as I said, all o' the coins are accounted for."

"Well, Paddy Finegan, if all of the coins are accounted for, there is no crime, is there?" the Queen asked.

"Your majesty." All eyes turned to Fionn as he rose to his feet. "Molly and Paddy came here from the real world. This coin, however, is from Glimmer. Through an accident, they have been pulled into Glimmer and it seems through time as well. I believe that Paddy stole this coin sometime in the future. That's why we have all of the coins now."

"What do you suggest, then?" asked the Queen.

"Put the coin into the Treasury. That way it will be there when Paddy steals it later. Of course, we can hardly prosecute Paddy for a crime he hasn't committed yet."

"He's a genius, that lad is," Paddy whispered in Molly's ear.

"Let it be so!" the Queen commanded. "Paddy was also instrumental in delaying Corrigan in the garden when Molly saved me — saved us all — from the Anamith. So I am told." She smiled at the leprechaun.

"And is Fionn really Prince in the kingdom now?" Molly asked. "Do you accept him as your son?"

"He is my son." The Queen looked at Fionn with a warm smile. "We have been separated for too long. It is time we got to know each other."

"Good." Molly nodded. "Now, I have one more thing to ask."

"Yes, child?" the Queen replied.

"Can you help me and Paddy go back home? I didn't bring my ruby slippers with me."

The Queen looked puzzled.

"Sorry," Molly said. "Inside joke."

"You didn't bring ruby slippers, but you did bring a leprechaun," Fionn said. "I have an idea, Paddy, when you have a few minutes?"

"And I may be able to help as well," the Queen said. "Lioc! Come here, my dear!"

A lovely young woman with flowing auburn hair and an azure gown stood up near the end of the table and curtsied. "Yes, your majesty?"

"Can you assist Molly and Paddy in returning to their own time?"

Lioc curtsied again. "I believe so, your majesty."

"Good! Then we need only one thing more!" the Queen glowed with satisfaction.

"What's that?" Molly asked.

"A rock nymph," Fionn grinned.

chapter nineteen

Lia Fáil

preparations quickly progressed for their departure the next day. Attendants cleaned Molly's clothes and Paddy polished her boots till they held a glowing luster. Paddy's suit was still in pretty good shape, but he picked out a new vest that he liked even better than the one he had gotten at the Exposition.

When everything was ready they were summoned before Queen Meb once more. Paddy bowed and Molly curtsied. Fionn stood proudly next to his mother. He nodded his head as he gave a big smile to the girl and the leprechaun.

"We have been blessed by your company," the Queen smiled. "Now it is our turn to return the kindness you have shown us. We will send a rock nymph with you who can take you from one rock to another with only a thought."

A short, pudgy fairy stepped forward. She wore a tunic that might have been made of rough cloth, or it could have been carved from stone. Molly couldn't be sure. "I'm Sandy," the fairy said with a shy grin. "I'm happy to be o' service."

"I'm glad to meet you, Sandy," Molly said with another curtsey.

"Sandy can move you from one rock to another, but that will not be enough to get you home," the Queen continued. "Lioc?"

The young woman from the banquet table the previous night stepped forward and curtsied to the Queen. She held a rolled parchment in her hand. "Your majesty, this scroll will aid its holder to move through time. Used in combination with the rock nymph's power to move through space, it should return our travelers to their home." She turned to Sandy and extended the scroll. "When the time comes, have Molly and Paddy each touch the scroll while you are holding it. Their thoughts will guide you to take them to the proper place."

"Thank you, milady," Sandy said humbly as she took the scroll.

"Mother, may I accompany them as far as I may?" Fionn inquired.

"I think that would be fine," the Queen smiled. "That's very thoughtful of you, my son."

"Well, I'm ready to go home. It's been wonderful meeting all of you even though I haven't enjoyed everything that's happened here! I'll never forget you!" Molly said as she shouldered her backpack.

"Well then," said Sandy as she took charge, "we just need a fairly good-sized piece o' rock to get us started. Fortunately, this entire castle is made o' rock. Everyone come over here."

Sandy tucked the scroll away in her tunic and placed one stubby hand against the wall. She reached out for Molly's hand.

"Aren't we supposed to touch the scroll?" Molly asked.

"Not yet. We have to make one stop first. We'll need to visit a special stone to get you out of *Fannléas* and through time. Molly, Paddy, Fionn, hold on to my free hand."

The three crowded together and grasped Sandy's outstretched hand. Molly looked around one last time at Queen Meb, sitting in regal splendor on her carved throne.

Then the world turned inside out.

Visions of crystals flashed in front of her eyes, blue and grey lights flashed around her, and she had a strange feeling, as if she was going to fall off of a chair that was perfectly safe. She grasped Sandy's hand tighter.

The strange lights vanished as suddenly as they appeared. Molly wobbled, but found her feet on solid ground. Sunlight streamed into the narrow hallway where the four stood. The rock in front of Molly had worn circular carvings in it. She traced the grooves with her finger, wondering how old they might be.

"All right, everyone outside!" Sandy ordered, and marched out into the sun.

They emerged from a low doorway. When Molly looked back she saw they had emerged from an earthen mound. The sun was in front of them, about mid-afternoon, Molly thought.

"Now where to?" Paddy asked.

"To the other side o' this mound," Sandy said cheerily. "It's as close as I could get us with enough rock close by."

They walked around the mound, glancing back at the low hill behind them. As they approached the north end a solitary stone came into view. It was tall and slender, rounded on top and about four feet in height. The ground around its base was bare.

"This is the stone?" Paddy said in amazement. "Oh, this is too good to be true!"

"What is it, Paddy?" Molly asked.

He turned to look at her excitedly. "This is the *Lia Fáil!* The Stone o' Destiny! We're at Tara!"

"The Stone of Destiny? The one you told me about before, that you never had the chance to visit? Paddy, that's so cool!" Molly looked at the stone, and then at Sandy. "Are we really going to use the Stone of Destiny to get back home?"

Sandy nodded. "This is one o' the four treasures of Ireland. It has great power."

The rock nymph strode up to the *Lia Fáil* and rested one hand respectfully on it. She pulled the scroll out of her tunic with the other hand. "Come on, now! You're very close!"

Molly and Paddy approached the stone. Molly could hardly contain her excitement at finally returning home. She reached out eagerly to touch the scroll, but something felt wrong.

She turned to see Fionn standing by himself.

"Fionn, aren't you coming?"

He smiled and shook his head.

Molly ran to the blond-haired boy and caught him in a tight hug. "Oh, Fionn, how can I leave you here? You're so — so …"

Fionn gently turned her face up to his. "Molly," he said softly, "If I hadn't met you, I would still be running away from the O'Doherty brothers or maybe back in their horrible house as a prisoner. I owe my life, the very meaning of my existence — to you. In my book you're the *fifth* treasure of Ireland. But Molly, I can't come with you. You belong in your world, and I belong in mine. You and Paddy have to go back alone." Then he slowly, tenderly, kissed her on her forehead.

Molly closed her eyes and buried her head in his chest. She didn't want to let go, even though she knew he was right. She looked up at him again. "Well, you're the one who ate the Salmon of Knowledge. You're right. I have to go home."

She stepped back, smiling through her tears, and then walked to the Stone of Destiny. She placed her hand over Paddy's on the little scroll and looked back at Fionn.

"Think of home, Molly," he smiled. "The scroll won't work right if you're not thinking of home."

Molly nodded and closed her eyes. "I'm ready," she said.

Sandy, Molly and Paddy vanished like a dust storm on the afternoon breeze. Fionn stood looking at the place where they had been for a moment, then walked over to the stone and sat down. He sat quietly for several minutes, listening to the wind blowing through the grass and the birds singing as they flew overhead.

He slowly extended his legs. As his feet touched the *Lia Fáil,* a growl rumbled from beneath the earth. Then a roar like a mighty lion defending his kill erupted from the stone as if it were a loudspeaker. The roar echoed over the hills, drowning the noise of the birds and the wind.

Fionn's expression did not change, and he let the sound sweep down from the hill for a few seconds longer. Then he pulled his feet back, leaving only the faint echoes of the roar to reverberate on the breeze until all was quiet and peaceful once more.

Fionn drew his knees up to his chin and wrapped his arms around them, staring at the stone for long minutes. Finally he stood, still looking at the *Lia Fáil.*

"I will try to be the best king I can be," Fionn whispered softly.

chapter twenty

The Way Home

Three figures appeared next to the *Lia Fáil* like synchronized swimmers breaking the water's surface without a ripple. A small red-haired girl and a green-suited leprechaun gently held a small scroll with one hand and maintained a vice-like grip on the third figure with their other hand.

"Ouch! Okay, already, let go o' my arm!" Sandy yelped. "We're here!"

Molly and Paddy sheepishly relaxed and took a step back. "Sorry, Sandy," Paddy said, "But ye have to admit that was quite a trip!"

Molly looked around her. The sun was just peeking over the horizon to her left. The Stone of Destiny was still there, but now buff-colored bricks formed a sunburst pattern radiating out from its base. The Irish countryside stretched green and rolling toward the horizon in the early dawn. "Look!" she called. "There's a sign here, a modern one! These bricks weren't here before … and we're on top of a hill! Where did the mound go?"

"It's behind us, Molly," Sandy said after looking around for a second. "Right down there. Someone must have moved the stone up to the top o' the hill."

Molly let that sink in for a second before she answered. "Then — we've moved through time? We're in our own time again, and in the real world?"

"I let your thoughts guide me, Miss. If your thoughts were true, then we are in the right place and time." Sandy smiled at Paddy. "And Mr. Finegan had some pretty strong thoughts on the subject as well!"

Paddy turned to Molly. "Rub your bracelet now, to make sure we're in the right place."

Molly rubbed the silver bracelet, feeling the lines of ivy and crescent moons glide beneath her fingers. Paddy nodded with satisfaction. "We're in the real world for sure. I hope that scroll helped guide us to the proper time as well."

He faced the little rock nymph. "Thank ye, Sandy, we're both grateful to ye," Paddy grinned. "Do ye think ye could drop us off closer to the Burren? It's a long walk from here."

"O' course." Sandy carefully tucked the scroll back into her tunic. "I'll be needin' that to get back home myself. Are there any rocks in this Burren o' yours, Mr. Finegan?" She winked at Paddy.

"Oh, here and there," he chuckled.

"Well, pick one out and think about it. Take my hand, both o' you, and we'll get you there. Just a short hop this time, Miss." Sandy gave Molly an encouraging look.

Molly and Paddy grasped Sandy's outstretched hand while the rock nymph rested her other hand once again on the *Lia Fáil*. When the visions of sparkling blue and grey crystals faded away, Molly saw that they were nearly surrounded by large upright slabs of limestone on either side, with another one above their heads that rested on the supports.

"Paddy, this looks familiar. Oh, I remember! Only there's no gold here now! This is the dolmen, isn't it?" Molly asked excitedly.

"That it is, Molly dear," the leprechaun smiled in delight. "I'd recognize these stones anywhere. Look, there's one o' Kevin's matches. If he's not careful, he's going to help some up and coming archeologist come up with a whole new theory."

"An archeologist? Isn't that a scientist who tries to figure out what kind of life existed in pre-historic times?" Molly furrowed her brow.

"Right again, Molly. Finding a leprechaun's match in a tomb thousands o' years old would make a great find." Paddy scooped up the burnt match and tucked it into his pocket.

"Well, I think I'll be gettin' back. It was grand making your acquaintances, milady, Mr. Finegan!" Sandy bowed slightly to them and pressed her hand to the wall.

"Wait!" Molly cried. "Aren't you going to take me back to Chicago?"

Paddy cleared his throat. "Actually, that will be *my* job. Thank ye, Sandy! Have a safe trip!"

Sandy vanished into the still air as Molly stared. "Paddy, how are you going to get me back home? I've got to get back to Dad!"

Paddy strolled out from under the dolmen into the dawn sunlight, whistling. Molly followed, looking ready to explode.

"Molly, remember when Fionn wanted to talk to me about somethin'?" Paddy asked.

"No," Molly replied crossly.

"He had an idea how I could get you back home. Fionn's rather clever, ye know."

"Yes, I know," Molly sighed. "Okay, what is this idea?"

"In a moment. First, I have to share somethin' with ye, now that we're away from the others."

Molly looked at Paddy closely. "Why couldn't you say this in front of the others?"

Paddy leaned close and whispered. "The only Queen I ever knew before we went to Glimmer was named Corrigan."

Molly sank to sit on one of the flat rocks that covered the area. "Corrigan? You're sure?"

"I don't think I'd be forgetting somethin' like that. Her name was Corrigan."

"But Corrigan is …"

"Dead." Paddy shook his head. "Because ye went in to protect Queen Meb from the Soul Eater, Queen Meb lived and Corrigan died at the hand of her own monster. If Corrigan had succeeded in her wicked plan …"

"Corrigan would have become Queen." Molly finished the sentence. She looked at Paddy in panic. "Paddy, I changed history! This could be terrible!"

"Oh, I don't know, Molly. This could be a very good thing. Anyway, it's done. I thought it best not to let the others know, seeing how it affected them directly."

Molly nodded. "That's probably a good idea. Paddy, I've been wondering. What if Work-dad isn't an idea that my father still has? What if Work-dad is an idea that's coming from *me?*"

The leprechaun gave a low whistle. "Faith, Molly, I hadn't considered that! If that be the case …"

"It doesn't matter. Either way, *I'm* going to have to deal with it. If it's my dad's idea, I have to talk with him about it. If it's my idea, I still have to ask him to know for sure that it's coming from me." She sighed. "Then I get to deal with *my* feelings about it. If I can change history, then I guess I can change this, too! If I can get home at all!"

Paddy smiled and reached into his other pocket. "Now, about getting ye back home."

Molly stared at the golden coin Paddy held in his fingers. "Paddy, I thought you were going to put that coin back into the Treasury! How could you steal from the Queen again?"

"Look at it carefully, girl. It's not the same coin."

Molly took the coin and saw that it had a picture of a man's head on one side and a harp on the other. "Okay, so it's a different coin. But the other coin was enchanted to take me back home!"

"Remember that the pouch was enchanted, too. The coin works when ye put it into the pouch."

"Did this coin come from the Treasury, too?" Molly remained dubious.

Paddy laughed, and his voice echoed across the Burren. "No, Molly, this coin is true leprechaun's gold!"

"Leprechaun's gold? That means that after a leprechaun gives it away …" Molly fell silent.

Paddy became very serious. "Yes, Molly, after a leprechaun gives it away, the gold disappears."

Molly looked at the little man and felt her eyes start to well up. She blinked the tears away fiercely. "A one-way ticket home."

"Aye." Paddy sighed softly and sat down.

"Well," Molly said, trying to keep her voice from cracking, "I suppose I'll just have to talk Family-dad into bringing us back for a vacation to Aunt Shannon's. A passport to Ireland is safer than a passport to Glimmer, anyway."

"I'll be waiting for ye, Molly. I'm way behind on me shoes these past couple o' months." He frowned. "At least, I think I am. If Corrigan was never Queen, did I really get thrown in prison?"

"We both have things to find out. Oh, Paddy, I've just got to make sure Dad isn't going back to the way he was before!"

"There's only one way to tell, Molly. Ye need to go now."

The girl bent to hug the elf tightly. Their eyes met for an instant. "By yourself, this time!" Paddy grinned.

Molly smiled and stood up. "Here goes, then! Hope to see you in a few months, Paddy!"

She dropped the coin into the worn leather pouch. Paddy watched as she vanished in a golden haze.

Molly felt her feet touch the floor and found herself in her bedroom. "I forgot to turn off the light?" she said out loud. She looked at her clock radio. *12:50 a.m. But what day, or what year for that matter?* She rushed to her computer and pulled up the clock function.

"Five and a half hours. I've only been gone for five and a half hours!" Molly sat back in her chair, shaking her head in disbelief. "I'm back, and they didn't miss me."

She noticed the leather pouch she had tossed on her bed in her haste to check the computer date. Retrieving it, she loosened the drawstring and pulled out the gold coin. "Was Paddy wrong? Can I keep this coin, too?"

But as she watched, the coin changed to glittering shards of light that flickered briefly and disappeared right out of her fingers. Molly sighed. There was no trace of the coin, any smudge or sign of it on her fingertips. The magic was gone.

She jumped as she heard a series of high-pitched beeps downstairs. A mechanical sounding voice said "Disarm system now!"

"I've got it, Kate," Molly heard her father's voice say as he shut off the alarm.

chapter twenty-one

The Right Thing

Molly didn't take time to think before she pounded down the stairs, thoroughly startling her parents.

"Oh, I've missed you guys!" Molly said as she locked her arms around her mother.

"Molly! We haven't been gone *that* long! Sean, maybe we left her alone sooner than we should have — she's positively shaking!" Kate squeezed Molly and stroked her hair.

"Why are you wearing your jacket, Molly?" her dad asked. "The heat didn't go off, did it?" He hurried over to the thermostat to check it.

"No, Dad, the heat's okay. I just got a little chill." *That was stupid, I should have taken my jacket off,* Molly thought. She looked at her mom. "I'm all right, Mom, really I am. I feel a lot more independent now than I did when you left. Trust me!"

"Well, that's good. I suppose we'll try leaving my little girl home by herself again some time. But only for a few hours!" Kate kissed her daughter on the forehead. Molly closed her eyes, remembering the last time she had been kissed there.

Sean O'Malley yawned and stretched. "It's one o'clock, people, time to hit the sack. I'm not much of a party person. Quite a spread of food the office had though, wasn't it, Kate?"

Molly turned from her mother and faced her dad. "I need to ask you something first, Dad."

"Can it wait until morning, pumpkin?"

"No." Her dad looked surprised at her tone. Molly continued, "I need to know, Dad. Do you still think about spending time at work away from Mom and me?"

He scratched his head. "Honey, I have to go to work, you know …" He paused as understanding lit his face. "Oh, I see what you're getting at. Let's sit down on the sofa for a minute."

They sat down next to each other. "Molly, do you remember when Mom and I came to get you at Aunt Shannon's this summer?" Molly nodded. "I said that I had been stupid, that I was giving up this road warrior crap — "

"Sean!" Kate scolded.

"— and I was going to be there for your mother and you. I took the regional sales job so I wouldn't have to take so much time away from you guys. I've done all that, haven't I, honey?"

"Yes," Molly said, "but don't you ever think about going back to the way you were sometimes? Traveling all around the world, making all of that money?"

Her father regarded her for a long moment, parsing her words. "Molly, I don't blame you for being worried that I might become a workaholic again. That's the way I was for years and years, it doesn't go away just like that." He snapped his fingers to illustrate. "I'd be lying if I told you I didn't think about those days sometimes."

"I knew it! I knew you were thinking about it!" She felt tears start to come again. "Dad, you promised!"

"Molly, listen carefully to me. This is important." Her dad took her hands and looked into her eyes. "Just because I have those thoughts doesn't mean I'm going to act on them. Honey, I struggle with those thoughts every day. And then I think about how much I love you and your mom, and I decide that I want to do the right thing instead of escaping to —" he smiled at Molly and winked, "— Hong Kong. Or wherever. Life is a series of choices, Molly. Everyone is faced with tough decisions in life. Sometimes making the right choice isn't easy to do at all. But life isn't about always doing the easy thing. It's important to do the right thing. I choose not to act like a workaholic, and I choose instead to give you and your mom the time you deserve. Yes, I am tempted to do the easy thing, maybe every day, and at the end of every day I thank my lucky stars that I choose to do the right thing when I come home to my family. Does that make sense, honey?"

Molly rubbed her eyes with her sleeve and nodded. "I think I understand about making tough choices, and doing what is right. I'm glad ..." she threw her arms around her father's neck and hugged him tightly. "I'm glad you want to do the right thing. Thank you for being honest." She sat back and looked at his face. "You trusted me enough to leave me at home by myself, and I need to trust that you will always choose to spend time with Mom and me. Although staying home all by myself turned out to be a lot harder than I thought it would be."

"You did just fine, dear," her mom said, coming over and hugging her shoulder. "Are you flushed, Molly? If I didn't know better, I'd think that you'd been getting too much sun."

"Really?" Molly put a hand to her cheek.

"Time for bed, everyone. Molly, you should have been in bed hours ago," her dad announced.

"One more thing, Dad. Can we go to Ireland this summer and visit Aunt Shannon?"

"You've been thinking about Ireland?"

Molly grinned. "Constantly!"

"I don't see any reason why not. We could drive on up north after we stop by Shannon's, maybe see Donegal."

"Yeah, it's so beautiful up there," Molly said dreamily.

"How would you know that?" her dad asked. "You've never been north of County Clare."

"Uh — maybe a leprechaun told me. Is there any place in Ireland that's not beautiful, Dad?"

Sean chuckled. "A leprechaun! I guess beauty is in the eye of the beholder. Ireland is a unique place, and much of it is quite beautiful. Now I think you'd better get to bed; you're getting ditzy!"

"I think I *will* go to bed," Molly yawned. "Goodnight!"

As she crawled under her blankets and waited for sleep to come, Molly's thoughts drifted back to Paddy. "I will come back and see you again, Paddy. I will." Then she closed her eyes and dreamed of castles, and princes, and a few things she didn't want to think about.

epilogue

Tales for Children

*t*hose who remember the old tales of Eire speak of a fairy known as Corrigan, who had a fondness for beautiful human children, and was blamed for all the changelings in the area.

The Queen of the Fairies was named Meb. Queen Meb had a son named Fionn, who was superbly gifted in his own right. He showed great wisdom beyond his years.

Fionn grew into a strong young man and a fearless leader. He was called Fionnbharr, or Finvarra, and became King of the Fairies. Unlike those who ruled before him, he was benevolent toward humans. Few knew why he favored the humans so much; it was whispered that a human had befriended him in his youth and he never forgot it. It helped shape him into the kind, caring ruler who brought joy to all in his kingdom.

Molly closed the book of *Irish Fairy Tales* and set it beside her. "Wow," she whispered to herself. "I wonder if Paddy knows? I'll have to ask when I see him this summer." Her hand rested briefly on the shimmering cloth lying on her bed, woven on the fairy looms of Tiarnach in the land of Glimmer.

author's note

Imagination can take you anywhere, it has been said. At least, I think someone said it. There comes a point, however, when you have to admit that sometimes truth is stranger than fiction.

Take for example Molly and Paddy's adventure into the Columbian Exposition. Real place. Actually existed. So did Uncle Dan, and young Frank, and Anton the sausage seller. Most everything in chapters three and four has its basis in fact.

That's where imagination kicks in. You can start with something real and use your imagination from there. Especially when reality begins with Ferris Wheel cars as big as houses.

Instead of just *reading* Irish fairy tales, you can be *part* of the story. You can meet with the actual characters.

And if you happen to be traveling with a leprechaun and a stolen magic coin, who knows? Maybe you could even *change* that reality.

Then again, how can you be sure that history *wasn't* changed? I think I'll just leave that last thought for your imagination.

glossary

Term	Definition
Alvaro Giovanni	An Italian human alchemist who was duped into helping the evil fairy Vroknar create the Soul Eater (*Anamith*). He was later locked away in Castle Dúr with his creation.
Anamith	The Soul Eater. Fatal to fairies, very nasty to humans.
Burren	A unique part of western Ireland with much limestone, many caves, and a wide variety of plants and flowers that grow there.
Cathair	A stone ringfort. Molly discovered a ringfort in the Burren.
Cillian	A human boy stolen by Corrigan and placed as a changeling in the cradle of the Fairy Queen's son. His name means "strife."
Daghda	One of the leaders of the fairies. His magical cauldron is one of the four treasures of Ireland.
Dúr	Means "dark." Castle Dúr therefore means "Castle of Darkness."
Eire	The gaelic, or Irish name for Ireland.
Fannléas	The Irish name for Glimmer, the fairy realm where ideas can become real.
Fionn	Queen Meb's son, who is replaced by a changeling. His name means "fair."
Gaelic	The old language of Ireland. Gaelic, or Irish, is now the official language of the country again, with English being a second official language.

Term	Definition
Gleoiteog	A mid-sized fishing boat of the Galway Hooker type. It is about thirty feet long.
Lia Fáil	The "Stone of Destiny" at Tara. It is one of the four treasures of Ireland.
Lioc	A young woman in Queen Meb's court who has some power over time.
Lugh	One of the leaders of the fairies. His spear is one of the four treasures of Ireland.
Meb	Queen of the Fairies, and Fionn's mother.
O'Doherty	The family who "adopted" Fionn. Means "hurtful."
Sidhe	The name for the fairy folk. It literally means "people of the (fairy) mounds" as the Tuatha dé Danaan fled underground after being defeated.
Tagnus	Gardner to Queen Meb.
Tara	Ancient capital city of the High Kings of Eire, and home of the *Lia Fáil,* one of the four treasures of Ireland.
Tiarnach	The castle where the Fairy Queen and her court live. The name means "Lord."
Tuatha Dé Danaan	The mythical people who became the fairies. From their four home cities they brought the four treasures of Ireland.
Vroknar	An evil fairy who helped create the *Anamith.* See Alvaro Giovanni.

Available from amazon.com
in print or Kindle format.

Duane Porter
Buried Treasure Publishing
2813 NW Westbrooke Circle
Blue Springs, MO 64015
(816) 210-4314

Books by Duane Porter:

Molly O'Malley and the Leprechaun

Molly O'Malley: Rise of the Changeling

Molly O'Malley and the Pirate Queen

Charlie and the Chess Set

The Seirawan Factor

The Best Ride

CPSIA information can be obtained at www.ICGtesting.com
Printed in the USA
LVOW01s1043070414

380618LV00001B/160/P